THE AMERICANS

JEANNE VRONSKAYA was born in Moscow, where she
graduated in Engineering at Technological Institute. She
worked for a short time as a French interpreter/translator
before turning to journalism. In 1968 she married a foreign
student-linguist and in January 1969 landed at Paris
Bourget airport. She lived in Paris and briefly worked at
the Renault Automobile firm as an engineer-interpreter
before she moved to London to join the BBC Russian
Service.
In 1972 Allen & Unwin published her first book in English,
a journalistic essay about the post-Stalin generation of
Russian filmmakers. From 1974 she worked as a freelance
journalist with a number of national newspapers, first
specializing in Russian affairs, mainly cinema, then turned
to writing extensive features for colour supplements. For
a time she was Russian affairs correspondent for Variety.
In 1979, the French publisher, Robert Laffont, published
her first novel, "Nous Etions Cinq" (We Were Five).
"The Americans" is her first novel translated into English.
Jeanne Vronskaya became a British citizen in 1977. Since
1969 she has been living in Knightsbridge, London.

Also by Jeanne Vronskaya

Young Soviet Film Makers, 1972, Allen & Unwin, out of print

Nous Etions Cinq, 1979, Robert Laffont, Paris

Jeanne Vronskaya

The Americans

Translated from the Russian
by
Barry Elliott

CHAGANO BOOKS
LONDON

Chagano Books
Special overseas edition published in 1984
by Chagano Books, 11 Connaught Place, London W2 2ET

First published in Great Britain by
Chagano Books 1984

ISBM 0 9509356 0 3

Made and printed in Great Britain by
Redwood Burn Ltd, Trowbridge, Wiltshire

NOTE FROM THE AUTHOR

The inspiration for this novel came from numerous visits I made to one of the many mental hospitals in the Moscow region in the 1960s. A friend of mine, who lives in Moscow today, refused to do his three years of military service.

I took food, drink and cigarettes to the hospital and in the visitor's room my friend recounted to me events he experienced. I was able to meet several inmates who are all featured in these pages. These men all wanted to leave the Soviet Union, which as this story shows, is considered to be a sign of mental illness. They were known by the hospital staff as 'The Americans'. These circumstances and this title still exists today.

Jeanne Vronskaya
December 1983, London

This story was written during the autumn of 1977 through to the summer of 1978. A translation of the first draft was undertaken by Barry Elliott in early spring 1979. Following revisions made by me in 1980, Russian-born Mrs Vera Dixon, re-worked the translation, and in 1981 Andrew Reynolds put colloquial English into the dialogue. In the summer of 1982 I revised some chapters and Mrs Sue Godfree kindly edited my revisions and re-typed the manuscript.

Jeanne Vronskaya
January 1984, London

FIRST DAY

I

I awoke to the feel of something cool against my burning face. Through a sort of haze I saw an old man stooping over me.

"You awake then, son? Right, let's just dab you again with this."

Into a mug of water on the floor he dipped a bit of cotton wool, squeezed out some of the water and pressed it to my head. At once I felt a sharp, shooting pain like a touch of hot iron, but this passed and the sensation felt quite pleasant.

"That's better; all you need is a dab of iodine for your lip and your nose. You stay here, I'll go and get it." He got to his feet with a groan, looked at me and then exclaimed.

"Ah damn, I'm a stupid old idiot, I should have untied you!"

Kneeling down again, he tried to ease me away from the wall, but I was too heavy for him to manage.

"Shift over a bit so I can get to you."

I began to turn over so he could get to my hands, tied behind my back, but I must have done it too abruptly. A terrible pain shot through me and I moaned.

"No, don't move your hands. They'll hurt, I know. Bloody bastards, beating a lad up so he can't even turn over. Take it easy, now, I'll soon have you loose."

He got a good grip on me and managed to turn me enough to get at my back. Carefully he began to undo the ropes binding my wrists. At last he had all the knots undone. I worked my arms and fingers to bring back the circulation but again felt a sharp pain.

"Easy, easy. Just move your shoulders till you get the feeling back. Are you thirsty, do you want a drop of water? I can get you some in a jiffy."

"Yes, some water would be good," I croaked. With the thought, a great thirst overcame me and I licked my parched lips.

The old man went out and I looked around. It was a white-painted, windowless room that was as empty as a shell; there was nothing, no furniture, not even a chair, just the white walls dimly lit by a bulb in a dingy shade high up on the ceiling. Fully conscious now, I propped myself up against the wall and saw everything again, how they had taken me.

It had been three in the morning and I was sleeping, tired after the day's work, when I realized dimly that somebody was hammering at the door.

"Parkin, open up! Police!"

I switched on the bedside lamp and went to open the door. Outside there were six men.

"What the hell is this?" They did not answer but rushed into the room and began to wade into me. Well, I hammered them back, and I bet we didn't leave a stick of furniture unbroken, but I was no match for six. Eventually they got my arms tied and somehow pulled on my trousers. My jacket they simply draped over my shoulders and buttoned it at the front. Then they dragged me, resisting all the way, past my scared neighbours, roused by the noise, down the stairs and out into the street, where they shoved me into the back of a van. The doors slammed shut. I picked myself up off the floor and sat down on a bench right opposite a middle-aged policeman, a sergeant. Through the barred window I could see into the driving cab occupied by three of the men who had seized me. The others must have gone off in a car which I had noticed near the van when they dragged me out. We drove on for about ten minutes, then suddenly our van slowed down and stopped.

"Are we there?" I asked the sergeant.

"I don't think so. Probably just picking up somebody else on the way."

He was right. Five minutes later we heard a series of piercing yells from a woman.

"Shits, creeps! I hope you all choke... damn you, you and your bastard kids! Drop dead, the lot of you!"

The van doors opened and the woman was shoved in to join us. She was young and fat, with flashing, angry-looking eyes. Her face was caked with make-up and she wore a tight grey skirt and a blouse cut so low that her enormous breasts were almost popping out. Seeing the sergeant she sneered, spat on the floor and sat down next to me on the bench.

"Got a fag, dear?"

"In my right-hand pocket. Get them yourself. My hands are tied."

She looked at my hands, half-hidden by the jacket and yelled at the policeman.

"Did you tie him up? You sod!"

"Calm down! It wasn't him."

She shut up at once and began to fumble about in my pockets for cigarettes.

"Where's your matches?"

"Look in my inside pocket."

She poked inside my jacket and I felt her large soft hands fumbling about my body. At last she found the box and lit up.

"Want one yourself?"

I nodded.

She fished another cigarette from the pack and sticking it in my mouth, leant against me to light it. Now her breasts were against my cheek and I could feel their warmth. The sergeant said nothing, but I could see him staring at them too. After a few pulls on her cigarette she began to examine me.

"Somebody been spoiling your looks, then, gorgeous?" she grinned.

"Trying to. What about you, what have they got you for?"

"I'm sick, dearie," she said bitterly. "I've got what they call an 'erotic-sexual psychosis'. Why are you smiling?"

"What the hell is that?"

"Well, I had a lot of johnnies coming round to see me, and a girlfriend of mine reported it."

8

"I get you."

"It's because the johnnies were all foreigners, Germans, Americans. They wouldn't have bothered if I'd stuck to our own, dirty Ivans. And that bitch was green with envy."

For some minutes after this we drove on in silence. She finished her cigarette, tossed the butt onto the floor, then turned to face me.

"You've got nice grey eyes, and I can see you're well built. As soon as you get away from *them*..." she glanced scornfully at the sergeant, "just come along to me. I'm always outside the Central Market of an evening, you know the Central Market, of course?"

She moved around until her breasts were pressing into my side and suddenly flung her arms round my neck.

"Cut it out! That's not allowed," snarled the sergeant.

"You fuck off! You're just jealous I'm not hugging you, you mangy old dog." And she clung even closer to me.

I could feel her breath hot on my neck and the life vibrant in her generous body. She began to kiss me, but that was too much for the sergeant who rushed over and tried to pull her away.

The woman let go of me, turned and with all her strength hit him in the face with her fist. They struggled together, swaying in the van, the woman yelling and cursing. The van stopped and the three other policemen dashed round from the cab and hauled her out into the road, where she continued to yell and fight like a tiger. In this melee she accidentally caught one of the policemen in the eye with her heel. He screamed, clutched his face and fell to the ground writhing. One of his mates

9

blew his whistle shrilly; soon a police Volga screeched to a stop and two more policemen jumped out. With their combined efforts they at last bundled the woman into the car and drove her away. A few minutes later another police car arrived and took the injured policeman. Then, the excitement over, the dishevelled sergeant resumed his place opposite me and we, too, left.

We drove for a good hour, the deserted streets of the city drifting past outside the barred van window like a dream. I was being driven somewhere. I could hear the whistles of departing trains and the clang of buffers. Then silence once more. Eventually we slowed down and turned off the main road. Through the darkness I made out some solid iron gates which I could hear were being opened and we then proceeded along a gravel drive. Shortly afterwards we stopped, the doors opened and the sergeant jumped out.

"Out you come!" he shouted.

I clambered out of the van, pain coursing through my shoulders and my whole body, and looked round. A flight of six stone steps led up to a sort of terrace and an open doorway in which stood three young fellows in white coats. I immediately realized where they had brought me.

"I'm not going in there," I said firmly.

The three men stood silent, watching me grimly from above.

"Why not?" asked the puzzled sergeant.

"Because I don't belong in a loony bin. Take me to the police station, if you want." I began to clamber back into the Black Maria.

"Come back here!" yelled the sergeant, grabbing me by the jacket. The buttons burst and the jacket fell off onto the driveway.

The three men in white coats seized me from behind and pulled me out of the van. They wouldn't have managed it so easily had my hands not been tied. One of them produced a sort of club from somewhere, hit me, and I remembered no more. Apparently after that they had simply dragged me into the building, dumped me in this room and tossed my jacket over my body. During the night I must have come to several times, because I could remember the walls and the ceiling swimming. And I could remember a pretty nurse giving me an injection. Or perhaps I dreamt it all? Then I must have slept until the old man woke me.

"What's the time?" I asked the old man when he returned, a bottle of iodine in one hand and a mug of fresh water in the other.

"Half past nine, son." He waited until I drank the water, then opened the bottle and began to dab my face with a piece of gauze wrapped round a spatula.

"Half past nine? Then why is it so dark?"

"It's night, not morning. You've been lying here all day. There now, I've fixed you up; I'll take you up to admin."

We left the room and walked down a long corridor, passing door after door before we finally stopped.

"In here."

The old man stayed behind the door and I went into the small front office. Through the door I could see a

11

fairly large, dimly-lit room. A tall man in a white coat was standing by the window with his back to me.

"Come in and sit down," he told me kindly.

I mumbled something like 'thanks' and sat down on a chair facing the desk and bolted to the floor like a cinema seat, a fact which I discovered on trying to shift it forward. He turned abruptly and I realized that this was no man but a middle-aged woman of very masculine proportions. From the white cap protruded a cluster of curls. Then the door opened and three orderlies came in. Two of them — husky and with the faces of criminals — took up station behind me. The third — I recognized him immediately — was the one who had knocked me out with his club. I took a closer look at him. He was thin with a curiously long, gaunt face. He was obviously senior to the others as he sprawled negligently in an easy chair next to the desk at which the masculine-looking doctor was now seated. He recognized me all right as he gave me a nasty grin.

"Rakoff, I don't need you," said the doctor in a voice in keeping with her looks. "And you can go too," she pointed to my escort.

The orderlies trooped out and we were left alone. The wall light showed up an ageing, unattractive narrow face. For some minutes she continued writing, then set aside her pen and began to scrutinize me as though I were some rare kind of beast.

"Well, now let's have a talk, Parkin," she said at long last. "Tell me about yourself."

"Should I stand up?"

"Stay as you are. I am listening."

"I wouldn't want to waste your time."

"It's all right. Tell me when did you begin to feel ill?"

12

"What do you mean? I've never had an illness in my life, not even flu. Look at me: I've got excellent teeth." I opened my mouth, bared my teeth and began to get to my feet, but she waved me back into my chair.

"Not a trace of baldness, and the women don't complain."

"Stop playing the fool, Parkin. I don't believe you're ill, I was just joking. Although I must say your behaviour is strange. What was it all about then?"

"I don't know what you mean."

Again I made to get up, and again she waved me back.

"Really? Look..." She opened a file. "You graduated from university in history and for three years before you studied philosophy, and yet you work as a lorry driver. Now that's odd, you must agree. Then in the past year you've been detained several times for drunkenness in public. You hit your boss at a meeting. What did you say when he told you off?"

"Nothing."

"Nothing? You used four-letter words in front of fifty people and you say you did nothing. And now there's the matter of the house. Tell me, why did you do it?"

"Just what have I done?"

"What have you done? Really, my dear fellow, have you forgotten? You took a bulldozer and demolished a newly-built house belonging to your friend. And then you resisted the police when they came to arrest you, so that they had to tie you up and bring you here by force. And right outside the door you started a fight and had to be subdued by our senior orderly. Can you explain all that?"

I saw there was no point talking to her, so I continued to play the fool and shook my head.

13

"What are you laughing at?"

"Because it's funny," I burst out.

Her thin lips tightened.

"All right. That's enough for today. You'll now be shown to your ward. Get all the rest you can here, and everything will be fine."

She pressed a button on her desk and got to her feet, displaying her angular frame.

I stood up too.

"Wait out there in the front office."

Unhurriedly I left her office, almost colliding in the doorway with another doctor, a young, attractive woman, whose face seemed vaguely familiar. As I sat on the bench in the next room I heard them talking; the walls were so thin I could overhear the whole conversation.

"It's very sad. A strange lad, that one. Take a look at his file," said the senior doctor. I heard the rustling of pages. "Where are we going to put him?"

"Thirty-Second Department is full up, they've got beds in all the corridors."

"Then let's put him in Forty Ward, Department Seven. When there's room we can transfer him to Thirty-Two."

"Ward Forty's full, but there's room in Thirty-Nine."

"Oh, Thirty-Nine. I don't know. We can't put him in Thirty-Nine Ward — all right, if we've no choice, Dementich!"

My old man got up from his seat in the corridor and went into the room.

"Dementich, take this young man to Ward Thirty-Nine."

"This way, son," said the old man in a friendly tone.

We walked down another corridor, turning left and right until we came to the bath-house. In the dressing room the old man turned me over to another orderly, a pock-marked character, and sat down to wait.

"Take your things off and get in the shower," came the order.

Obediently I undressed and padded into a shower room. The orderly followed me, sat down on a stool in the corner and fished an apple from his pocket. I stood under the gurgling shower, trying to clear my mind. The orderly stared at me, idly nibbling his apple. Bloody pouf, I thought, and turned away.

In came a middle-aged, naked man, unshaven, with eyes that seemed to burn. He took the stall next to me — twisting, frantically rubbing himself, grunting — never still. Noticing me only added to his frenzy. He winked, then glanced nervously at the pock-marked orderly, who stared dully at us and munched away at his apple. The man leant over to me and hissed:

"Do you want to get out of here?"

"What do you want?" I snarled.

"Well, this is what we do. We finish our wash and it's straight to the airport. I've got a plane standing by for take-off. Only — psst!" He put a finger to his lips and nodded towards the orderly. Suddenly he began to buzz like an aeroplane.

"Zzzzz... Time to take off."

"Shut it!" the orderly said lazily.

"Zzzzz..."

"I told you to shut it, you bugger!"

"Zzzzz... Gaining height... Five thousand metres... Zzzz..."

The orderly tossed aside his apple core and stood up.

"Shut your fucking mouth when I tell you, you scum!"

"Coming in to land, zzzz... Landing, bummm.."

The sound was cut off abruptly as the orderly waded into him with his fists, grabbed hold of his arm and dragged him out of the shower. The man made no resistance but continued his buzzing. When I came through into the dressing room they had taken him away.

"Used to be a pilot," explained old Dementich.

"Who was?"

"Well, him, of course, the zizzer."

Through a window a scruffy old woman handed me some rag of a towel, a striped baggy garment she called pyjamas, and a pair of slippers that had seen much better days. I dressed and looked at myself in the clouded, cracked mirror on the wall. God, I looked dreadful! My face all cut up, a great black bruise under my right eye, a split lip all smeared with iodine. Any scarecrow looked better.

The pock-marked orderly came back, took my clothes together with my money, the keys to my apartment and my pen and handed them to the old woman. I needed the pen and I asked for it back.

"It's not allowed."

All they left me was my watch, a comb, a hankerchief, a blank notebook and a packet of cigarettes. But they took the matches.

"Shit... How can I smoke without matches?"

16

"Shut up... Matches aren't allowed. You can get a light from the orderlies."

Silently I clutched Lika's ring which I had slipped off my finger when I guessed they might take it away. The orderly disappeared. He returned soon after with an inmate, who undressed and I could see that tattoos covered his chest, his arms, his legs, and even his belly: mostly lips and other parts of the female anatomy. His belly was decorated with a female face with two large eyes and long eyelashes. He saw me staring, flexed his belly muscles and made them wink, first one eye and then the other.

"What are you in for this time, Simon?" asked my old orderly.

"Ah, nothing really. Tried to fuck some bitch who turned out to be a member of the party." Simon's laugh filled the bath-house.

"Get on with you, you didn't!" exclaimed the old man.

"I swear it's true, grandpa."

2

"What's this Ward Thirty-Nine like, Dementich?" I asked when the pock-marked orderly had taken Simon into the bath-house, and the old woman at the window had disappeared.

"It's special; good one. For healthy loonies who want to go to America. We have a few whose mother or father is a foreigner. They dream of joining them but aren't allowed to. There are also some Jews. They want to go to America too; they don't have anyone there but insist on America all the same. We have a few Germans. They, naturally, want to go to Germany. We don't have politicals here, only one at the moment. They threaten him with insulin treatment but he hits back with Marxism. Thin as a rake, but the passion in him! His eyes all gleaming, and as clever as Marx himself. To talk to, he's a walking cyclopaedia..."

"You mean they put him in here for Marxism?" I asked in disbelief.

"Of course, what else? He was showing them proper Marxism and they didn't like that at all. Anyhow, they put you in here for anything nowadays."

The old man sighed.

"Do you know what insulin treatment is?"

"No."

"It's a death sentence, I can tell you. They bring a man in here, a genius, as sane as you are, and then addle his wits with that insulin. It's all Loza's job..."

"Who's that?"

"The Head of Department. You'll be seeing him, such a cultured type to look at, but chief assistant to the Devil himself. Talks real nice to you, too, but he'll send you off to the Insulin Room in a flash. Does experiments on people, he does. And Petters, she's a senior doctor, the one you just saw. She's a proper witch. You don't get many good ones here. Who wants to work as a fascist, eh?"

"You said Loza is assistant to the devil. So who's the boss here, in case I want to complain?"

"The boss, he's up there," the old man pointed to the

18

ceiling. "The likes of us don't get to see him. And as for complaining, there's nobody to complain to. I hear you work as a philosopher, son — or have I got it wrong?"

"How do you know that?"

"Oh, you can hear everything that goes on in that room from out in the corridor. Even when you don't want to."

"Well, I'm not a philosopher. I used to study it at university, but I chucked it in. I work as a driver now."

"It's an honest job that, driving a lorry. You do people some good that way, shifting freight and people. You'll be all right. As soon as they get themselves sorted out, they'll let you out, back to your lorry. It's not as if you're a political or want to go to America."

"No, I don't want to go to America."

We set off again down the long corridors, but now they were dotted with doors that the old man opened with his jangling bunch of keys. The doors slammed to on short, powerful springs. We got to a corridor with the offices of doctors and other medical staff and stopped at one marked "Department Seven, Ward Thirty-Nine." For the last time the old man opened a door. It slammed shut behind me; the sound went right through me.

"Wait here, son. I'll go and see if they've made up your bed and everything."

He left me by the door and shuffled off. I began to look around. It was a large corridor, about fifty metres long and fifteen wide with four large windows and several benches along the walls. Opposite the door through which we came in was another with the sign "Treatment Room." Between these two another door led to a Recreation Room. At the end of the corridor was the ward itself and next to that were what must be the toilets, to judge by the constant coming and going of people dressed like me in striped, baggy pyjamas. Several people stood smoking by the window and these turned to look at me with some curiosity. The old man came back and seemed to sense my mood, for he nodded sympathetically.

"Don't get worked up, son. Things'll work out, you'll see. God will keep you safe. Strewth, why don't those devils let useful folks alone to get on with their life?"

In the ward there was the thick acrid smell of sweat and tobacco; in fact there was such a fug of smoke that it was some time before my eyes adjusted and I could see anything at all. Then through the murk I made out a large room with beds lined up close to each other, so close that for a moment they seemed like one enormous bed with men of various ages sprawled or sitting all along it. People were constantly jumping over the low bed ends. In contrast to this huddle, the centre of the ward was an expanse of open space, criss-crossed by figures wandering about as though in some sort of trance.

Up bounded the strangest creature — a dwarf, seemingly getting on in years although, as I later found out, actually a few months younger than I. He had a small, egg-shaped, shaven head with a nose out of all proportion.

"Over here, this is your bed," he croaked in a hoarse voice from about the level of my waist.

Fascinated, I examined this weird combination of child's body, shaven tiny head and huge nose.

"Excuse me, are you an American?"

"What do you mean, American? I'm Russian."

"Well, of course you are. All of us here are Russians. I mean what are you in for?"

At this point two men came up. One, a broad-shouldered handsome lad of about my height. Even intense proletarization could not wipe from his features traces of good birth and breeding. The other was not that tall, but thick-set, fair hair, with a face showing indestructible good health.

"I suppose you tried to get out to the West, too," continued the inquisitive dwarf.

"I don't know what you're on about," I retorted, although I already knew something from the old man, but I had no intention of letting him know that, or telling him anything about myself. The only thing was his manner was so polite that I couldn't bring myself to tell him to clear off.

"What did they get you for?" asked the tall lad seriously.

"Oh, nothing really. I was just settling a score with somebody," I answered grudgingly.

"I get you, but it looks like they settled one with you too," the fair-haired one laughed, examining my beat-up face.

"We thought you must be an American too", sighed the dwarf.

"Knock it off, Robert. He doesn't know what you're on about," the tall lad said to the dwarf. "My name's

Max Whitley, and he..." pointing to the fair-haired, "he's Rolf Hartmann..."

They lined up to shake hands.

"Parkin. Boris Parkin," I introduced myself.

Max then repeated, with many details, what the old man had told me, that I had got into the special ward, filled mainly with those who wanted to leave the country and get abroad, mostly to America, so that — regardless of their actual destination — they were all called *Americans*.

"Is that why you all have American names?" I laughed.

"Of course," confirmed Max. "And from now on you're Bob, not Boris..."

Max had the bed next to me on my left, and that was all to the good because the bed to my right was occupied by a tall, hefty-looking character with a scared look on his face and his head pulled down into his shoulders, and a hairy chest. On his knees he was rocking a doll. Seeing me staring Max said:

"That's Leon. Crazy as a cuckoo but harmless. He's been here for three months. You'll be all right with us, we've got quite a good crowd in here, really. Now Robert..." he pointed to the dwarf, "he's a Circus performer..."

At the mention of his name the dwarf delivered a sweeping, artistic bow.

"And Rolf, he was shortly to be an engineer."

"Max is a translator," added Rolf.

"But for the time being you're all Americans," I said.

We all laughed. In the doorway appeared the good-looking doctor I had seen in Dr. Petters' office, but it turned out she was not a doctor at all but a senior nurse by the name of Vera Cabot. Still her face seemed vaguely familiar.

"Anybody who wants a sleeping pill come to the Treatment Room," she announced, glancing at me.

Many of the men jumped up from their beds.

"I wouldn't mind some of that... Cor, I bet she's got a beautiful pussy..." one lad shouted after her.

At this point Max grabbed him by his pyjama jacket.

"Keep your fucking mouth shut."

It was Simon, whom I recognized as the tattooed type I had seen in the shower-room. He managed to tear himself loose from Max's grip and went to the far end of the ward.

"What the fuck is it to you, American? Think I'm pawing your bird, do you?"

"Shut your trap, you prick, I said, or I'll shut it for you."

"Come on then, just you fucking well try!" Simon started advancing to the centre of the ward.

I noticed he was clutching a pen-knife he'd managed to hide away somewhere, and I warned Max. But before Simon could take another step Rolf Hartmann edged up behind and knocked him flying with a sweeping chop of his hand.

"You cunts, bleeding fuckers..." wailed Simon, struggling to his feet.

Max tripped him up, pinned him to the ground with his knee and took away the knife.

"Let me go," groaned Simon.

"Shut the fucking noise. It's me the Count telling you!"

This new voice emerged from somewhere through the haze of tobacco smoke.

The silence was immediate. Heads turned and, following them, I saw on the furthermost bed, right in the corner, a youth, with an arrogant face; the nose had at some time been broken.

"It was the American who started it!" complained Simon tearfully.

"The Yank was quite right," the stripling silenced him.

"Let him go, Whitley," said Rolf.

Max, a fellow of considerable strength, hoisted Simon effortlessly to his feet.

"OK, you prick. Hartmann says to let you go, but listen. You try making passes at the nurses again and you'll get your arms broken."

Simon vanished through the door and we — Max, Rolf, and the dwarf — gathered on my bed.

"Simon just can't let a skirt alone. They brought him in just before you; attempted rape again," said Rolf.

"I met him in the showers. Who's the Count?"

"Yank!" drawled Rolf in imitation. "He's a criminal pretending to be a loony and nicknamed "the Count". He's got no interest in women ever since he got a knife in his balls in a fight. They say he was six months in hospital."

Suddenly came a soft whistle and someone hissed:

"Look out, Rakoff's coming!"

Everyone rushed to their beds, except the Count and his pal, a strapping Asiatic type with a black moustache setting off a brick-red face.

"Get into bed, quick," hissed Max.

I was just pulling up the bedclothes when the already familiar Rakoff appeared. The orderly looked just the same as he had an hour ago in Dr. Petters' office, except that in his hand he held the equally familiar club. I could see now that it was well about one metre long and bound at the top with leather.

"Not asleep, yet, scum?" he yelled from the doorway, ignoring the two card players completely.

The orderly walked between the two rows of beds, now and then striking out at people's legs.

"What are you sticking your tootsies out for? And you, you sod, where've you stuck your filthy rags? I've told you before I want them at the head of the bed."

"But there's no bed-side table to put them on," came the timid reply.

"What? You want bed-side tables? Do you want a poke in your ugly mug, too?"

Rakoff leapt round the foot of the bed and delivered a smart crack on the offender's head. A heavy one, because we heard the groan. Then he came to my bed.

"You want a bed-side table, too? And what are your fucking slippers doing in the middle of the room?"

He yelled and brandished his club but held back from striking. He knew I remembered him; now he was alone, my hands weren't tied and he guessed I'd fight back.

"The lad's new," said Max.

"I couldn't care a fuck if he's new. I want order. Eleven o'clock, everybody sleeps."

"May I say something?" timidly asked an old man.

"What's that? Anyone who wants to talk to me should bloody well keep quiet. Well, what do you want, you old windbag?"

"I just wanted to draw your attention to the fact that it's not eleven yet, it's only twenty to..."

"Shut your trap, you piece of shit. I'll show you 'not eleven'. If Rakoff says it's eleven, it's fucking eleven..."

25

For a while longer the orderly paced about the ward, menacing the inmates with his club, then abruptly left the room. Behind him leisurely trooped the Count and his friend, the mustached Tartar Musa.

"They'll be up boozing and playing cards half the night," said Max.

"How can they, in a hospital?"

"Oh, the orderlies here booze with criminals all the time. But we can't. If they catch us at it, they stick you in the Violent Wing."

"Why do they keep criminals in with the sane patients?"

"So they can terrorize the politicals, although apart from Krivin, the Marxist, there's not a single political here. We're all here on false charges, but they class us as politicals."

"Let's get some sleep," said Rolf, who had the bed on the other side of Max.

"We get up early here," Max whispered to me.

We wished each other good night and I settled down to sleep. At once a dreadful fatigue came over me; my head was like lead, my body all weak. The odd light that was left burning did not bother me at all. I fell asleep.

3

I don't know how long I slept, but I woke to a piteous cry. At first I had no idea where I was. I opened my eyes. The light was on and I witnessed a horrible scene. Rakoff, the orderly, was leaning over the foot of the bed, gripping the dwarf by his shoulder and belabouring his back with the club. The dwarf was yelling:

"Please, please... It's only 'David Copperfield'! I have permission for it."

"What? 'David Copperfield'! It's something Jewish? I'll teach you to read Zionist literature..."

On the floor lay a book, or rather the remains of it, torn to shreds. I leapt out of bed, but what came next happened so quickly that I had difficulty afterwards piecing together the whole sequence of events. I think I just grabbed him and threw him out of the door, because I could recall something heavy thudding in the corridor. The dwarf stopped his yelling and looked at me with gratitude mixed with amazement. Everybody jumped out of their beds and crowded round us, except — as Rolf told me later — the Count and Musa, who pretended to sleep through all the din.

"Wow, that was some throw! You ever play basketball?" asked Max in tones of respect.

"A bit, but that was ages ago. It's a long time since I did anything more than handle a steering wheel..."

They all laughed. Rakoff didn't come back to the ward and in a while we got back into our beds. It was still only two o'clock in the morning.

"He'll try and get his own back as soon as he can," Max warned.

"We're quits now," I grinned.

Later I woke up again with a dreadful urge for a cigarette. As quietly as I could I slipped out of bed and went out into the corridor. That evening Max had given me a box of matches.

I went to the window and lit a cigarette. It was getting light. Suddenly I heard a stifled laugh. The door to the

27

Treatment Room was slightly ajar, and in the narrow chink of light I saw Max. One arm round her waist, he was busy kissing Vera Cabot, the attractive nurse. She tried to break free, or anyway pretended to and laughed. Now I remembered why her face was so familiar: it was she who had given me the injection the night I was brought in. Quickly I moved away from the door, took a couple of drags on my cigarette, tossed in into a can and slipped back into the ward. About half an hour later Max returned, but I pretended I was asleep.

SECOND DAY

I woke in the morning to loud singing. My watch said a quarter past six.

"Pay no attention: it's just the Count doing his nut," Max raised himself slightly on the bed and reached out for his cigarettes.

"He's got this routine — starts off the morning singing. The only way to shut the bastard up would be to beat his brains out. Go back to sleep; breakfast's not till eight."

Max fished a book from under his pillow and began to read, soon completely absorbed. I could see it was a thick, tattered English-Russian dictionary and remembered Rolf saying yesterday that Max was a translator. Max looked up and saw me watching.

"In an American ward like this I'm afraid of forgetting all my English."

I slid right down under the bedclothes and tried to get back to sleep, but the Count was making such a din that sleep was hopeless, besides which the criminals —

the Tartar and Simon — had started a brawl.

"You've got to see it his way, the bastard. He doesn't want to go back to prison; he's much better off here."

Max tore himself away from his dictionary.

"The doctors know he's doing his nut. But they need him." I looked at him in amazement. "You'll understand everything later. Ah, old Leon's awake. Morning, Leon! How's things?"

Leon was sitting up in bed, a lanky figure, clutching his doll. "Hello," he mumbled looking scared. "Who might you be?"

Again the same timid face, the head pulled right down into the shoulders, the hairy body shrinking as though from some expected blow.

"I'm Max. Max Whitley. Don't you know me, Leon, old friend?" Max laid aside his dictionary.

"Know what he weighs? Guess? Ninety kilograms. I weighed him myself just a week ago, and his height is nearly 2 metres. He's as strong as an ox but the criminals and the orderlies beat him up whenever they get the chance. Leon, don't you know me?" Max came round my bed and sat on Leon's.

"I know you. I remember you." Leon bounced up in bed so the springs groaned. "You gave me a prick yesterday."

"See, he doesn't remember a bloody thing. His memory's just about nil."

Max turned back to him.

"I didn't give you a prick, Leon. That's the orderlies. I'm Max, and we've been together nearly three months now..."

"No, no, no! I saw you yesterday, you gave me a prick." Leon insisted.

30

"It's hopeless," Max said to me over his shoulder.

"Leon, let's have a game of cards — whist or pontoon or something..."

"I don't have time. I've got to go and do peepee, and then I've got to get Ninochka washed. It's a hard day today, a lot to do..."

Sleep was now quite out of the question, so I decided to go out and stretch my legs in the corridor. On a chair by the window sat a youth with dark curly hair and a face with skin as smooth as any girl's. On his knees he balanced an album in which he sketched, glancing now and again through the window. I had a look — they were evidently rough sketches for a later painting. I could see a dog and an orange, a tree and a boy in silhouette, a flower and a cow, all strikingly done though they were only pencil sketches. Where did he get his subjects from in a gloomy place like this? I liked what he had drawn. I moved away so as not to disturb him. Absent-minded I stood by the window, toying with Lika's ring. Had I done the right thing, I wondered? It was all so long ago and there was no getting Lika back. No, I was right; the bastard had it coming. I had no regrets about that. I twisted Lika's ring on my finger and thought: this is all you have left.

The morning was grey and overcast, the sky swathed as though with some dingy curtain. Through the window I could see part of the yard, a fairly large square bounded on two sides by a mesh fence twice the height of a man, while the other two sides abutted on to our block, just one of several set in extensive parkland. The park was very large with a great many trees, also liberally dotted with statues of muscular women and men of equally subhuman appearance and if one screwed up one's eyes the statues seemed an emanation of the sick imagination of some artist, who could well have been one of this hospital's patients. I closed my eyes, then opened them to get rid of this nightmare. From my second-floor window I could also see a stretch of road beyond the wrought-iron gates and the fence, a long metal thread suspended in the grey murk. Somebody tugged at my trousers from below, and turning I saw the dwarf I had saved last night.

"Good morning, Bob, how did you sleep?" he enquired politely.

"Morning, Robert. Not too well, I'm afraid. I'm not used to it here."

"I've been here eight months," he looked sad, and his flabby little cheeks trembled.

"What are you in for?" I asked sympathetically.

And this was his story. During the war his mother, a young Russian girl (incidentally, of quite normal stature) was taken by force to Germany to work. When the war ended she landed up in France and soon after that got married.

"My father is a real Marquis", the dwarf assured me.

"Of course, here they gave me my mother's name".

Robert's French father didn't play the husband for

long. He seemed to have been an utter pervert, gambler and, alcoholic. Robert was born, indebted for his short stature to God knows whom, perhaps, as it later transpired, his father's dreadful ancestry.

Shortly after his birth, so as not to discredit herself with her new boyfriend, also French, through this freak of nature, his mother placed the poor boy with another French family far away in the country. Then, she persuaded some Russian friends who were returning to Moscow to take the ten-year old dwarf with them. There he was immediately given Soviet citizenship and three years later fixed up with a job in a circus. Before long he learned to speak Russian properly and had stayed with the circus until quite recently. His cherished dream, he told me, had been to find his mother. After ten years he got hold of her address and began to write to her, but this correspondence stopped abruptly when the little Marquis asked his mother to get him back to his native France. He reckoned this was the hand of the KGB. Robert was very persistent and began to haunt the French Embassy. This was not at all to the KGB's liking and one day they picked him up in the street just as he came out of the Embassy and brought him here. The diagnosis was 'mild schizophrenia from hereditary factors and a persecution complex', since the dwarf would insist to all the examining doctors that he was a French Marquis and that the KGB had stopped his mother's letters.

"Maybe just once in a lifetime those bastards weren't responsible," said Max later. "His Mum just abandoned him and stopped writing as soon as she heard he wanted to come back. At any rate, that's what his girlfriend, another dwarf at the circus, told me. And she got it from a friend of his mother's who was over here in Moscow on a tourist trip."

Max and Rolf came out and joined us, and we stood smoking in the corridor.

"We ought to introduce you to Alyosha, our artist," said Max.

We went up to the curly-headed youth I had seen sketching earlier.

"Alexei, this is Bob Parkin," said Max. "He only came in yesterday, but I feel he's one of us."

"Alyosha," said the lad, continuing to draw. "Alyosha junkie." Then, he laughed. "You don't believe me? Well, ex-junkie anyway. The only person in the American ward who's here of his own free will."

"That's true," Rolf chimed in. "He admitted himself."

"And you can leave of your own free will?" I asked.

"Certainly. I'm signing out after May Day. I'm through with drugs. It's a mug's game — always chasing after heroin, and the police always chasing you. And the money it's cost! Not to mention that I've nearly kicked the bucket a couple of times."

I looked at him closely and noticed that his lips were completely blue. He caught my look.

"I did that, I chewed them to ribbons when I came in here. I was so desperate for a fix I thought I'd die. I couldn't take it. Then I got over it; they cured me."

We were summoned to the canteen and Alyosha dashed off with his sketch-book, a small thin figure.

"He's real good lad," said Max. "And he's got great talent."

"Tell him he's a queer too, if you want to give him the full picture," muttered Rolf.

"So what?" retorted Max, "I don't give a fuck he's a

34

queer. He's never pestered me and he doesn't force himself on people."

4

We formed up and filed into the canteen, which was already occupied by another ward.

"Ward Forty, Suicides," explained Max. "Seventh Department that we're in has only got two wards — ours and the Fortieth. Most of those in Forty are lads who wouldn't do their army service, or else they were called up and did anything they could to get out. They hang themselves, slash themselves, anything. It's the only way they'll class you as unfit to serve and give you your ticket. They've got some ordinary suicides, too, of course; people who tried to kill themselves because they're alcoholics or got domestic troubles; students, usually from the humanities studying history or philosophy, and all disillusioned. They see no sense in life, just deceit everywhere. They wouldn't let the German, Pyotr Dutschke, go to Germany so he slashed his wrists in protest, and Misha, Mike Kauffman, Jewish, also protested: he cut his fingers off on his right hand. Of course, Forty Ward's got some genuine loonies and criminals too, just like we have."

The tables were set some distance apart. Our group — Max, Rolf, Robert and I — occupied one along with Leon, rocking his doll in his lap. Stooped as he was, he still towered above the rest of us.

Breakfast was a mug of what they called tea — a warm, cloudy liquid with a few black specks floating about — two chunks of bread, a small pat of marge and something in a dish. A strange yellow colour and semi-liquid, it looked quite inedible. I swallowed down the tea and bread but pushed this mess away in disgust.

"Eat up, you'll get nothing else," warned Rolf.

"I can't. I just can't stomach that."

"There'll be nothing else."

"I still can't eat it."

"Eat your porridge, Bob," the dwarf urged with a friendly smile.

"I can't," I repeated angrily.

"Leave him alone, Robert. In a day or two he'll be hungry enough to scoff anything," said Max.

Rolf ate up all my porridge and scraped the dish with a crust of bread. Next to me Leon quietly fed his doll. When he had finished he pulled out a handkerchief, gently wiped her mouth and laid her flat on his lap.

"Ninochka's had her feed. Now she has to sleep," he whispered to me.

Breakfast passed off calmly enough, except for a fight between the criminals — this time, ours and those of the Suicides ward headed by the Gipsy. He was as black as a raven and with a piercing savage voice. The fight was quickly stopped by the orderlies with the help of their clubs. Another incident took place when some loony crept up behind Leon and tipped a dish of porridge over his head.

"That's the Prophet", said Max. "Crazy as hell."

Leon slumped even lower, drew his head further still into his shoulders and began to weep, clutching his doll to his chest. The orderlies dragged the Prophet, laughing wildly, out of the room.

I left the table hungry as a hound. Robert gave me two apples, and a bar of chocolate. I tore into the juicy white flesh of an apple, savouring its fragrant aroma. I ate the whole lot, core and all, munching up the pips which were bitter but pleasant to the taste. Just think! Before this I had never bothered particularly with apples, rather disliking them, in fact, and never took one when offered. Now, with the apples and chocolate inside me, I felt perfectly content.

"Soon they'll be switching on the music and starting treatment," said Max gloomily.

"They'll not be treating him," Rolf nodded at me. "They won't have had any instructions about him yet."

"He's here by mistake," the dwarf said.

I didn't need telling I was in Ward Thirty-Nine by mistake. I'd heard Dr Petters telling Cabot that there was no room in Department Thirty-Two, where they'd meant to put me. Now I realized how lucky I was to fall in with the 'Americans' because the Thirty-Second, though more leniently run, was filled with alcoholics, real loonies, and criminals.

"We're all here by mistake," said Rolf.

They told me their stories. Max's father was one of a very small number of Americans who'd lived in Moscow since the 30's and survived Stalin's purges. After the war he married a Russian girl, his secretary-interpreter, thirty years younger than himself. He had died quite recently. Max longed to go to America to find his grandparents. He spoke English perfectly and, like his mother, worked as an interpreter. But as soon as he let it be known he wanted to go to America, he was immediately fired, and when he started meeting American tourists they brought him here.

Apart from three Germans — Hesse, Dutschke and Mayer — all from Kazakhstan, from families deported by Stalin at the beginning of the war from the Volga region, Rolf Hartmann was only half German through his father, a POW, who after the war met and fell in love with a Russian woman. They were refused permission to marry, even when Rolf was born. Then, Rolf's father was allowed to go to East Germany. There was some correspondence which suddenly stopped after a letter arrived not from East but West Germany, from Hamburg. That was already a long time ago. Rolf had lived with his mother and had always considered himself Russian until he met Linda, an American student who came to Moscow on a cultural exchange. They began to go out together and eventually he proposed. Unwisely, the girl blabbed about it to some 'girlfriend' in the same department of the university. Soon afterwards the KGB suggested to Rolf, that he stop seeing this

'American spy'. Linda was immediately expelled from the country and Rolf publicly announced himself German and started to look for his father's whereabouts, learned German and English, and when he started associating with Germans landed up here in the American Ward. Now he had no-one in the Soviet Union since his mother had died recently from cancer. He was very strong, handsome and reserved.

I was told that five Jewish lads had recently landed up here. Three of them were Muscovites: Victor Kotik, Vic, Mike Kauffman from the Suicides Ward, and Marc Lerner. They had tried to get out of the country legally and go to America but when they were refused permission they started going to foreign embassies for help. The other two from Odessa, Stolper and Volsky, had just been admitted. They had also been dragged in here for seeking help from foreign embassies.

I learnt that we had three criminals in our ward: the Count, Musa, and Simon. There were some genuine loonies, mainly quite mild ones like Leon and one engineer, who was in a state of deep depression. There was some scientist with a severe case of overwork; two truth-seekers and one chronic complainer. Oh yes, and Alyosha, the ex-junkie. The rest were sane Americans like Max, Rolf and me.

In the Treatment Room at ten o'clock I saw our senior nurse, Vera Cabot, with whom Max and all the Americans were in love. Now I could examine her. She was really a beauty, also very young. She had probably come here straight from Nursing School. Slim, with a shock of thick, reddish hair, a white face with a snub nose and large blue eyes — she set all the Americans atremble. Through the glass of the hatch I could just see her slender, well-groomed fingers and a strip of white neck with its little dimple above her collar. With a bored look she was issuing little plastic cups with pills, quite unconcerned as to whether the patients swallowed the medicine or not. Not like Petters, who would look into your mouth or arsehole for that matter. Max told me all this. With Vera Cabot on duty, if you didn't want to take your pills, you didn't even bother to put them in your mouth; you put them straight in your pocket to throw out later. It was this, as well as her looks, that endeared Vera to the Americans.

Before me in the queue for medicine stood Leon, as always clutching his doll which he carried day and night. He took a pill, smiled, put it on his tongue, swallowed it and licked his lips. Such a strapping lad — surely no pills could have any effect on him.

"More..." he begged.

Cabot smiled. Her teeth were as white as those of any toothpaste ad.

"No more, Leon. You're only allowed two."

She is, of course, an angel, compared with Petters and Rakoff. Now it was my turn. She recognized me at once.

"Parkin, isn't it?" This in a very velvety voice. The simulation of affectionate concern was obviously part of her duties.

"You only came in yesterday. There's nothing for you yet. The doctors will be taking a look at you next week."

She looked at me softly, the little pussy cat. Now I could understand why she was the talk of the Americans. She was hot stuff, and she knew it.

5

We — Americans and Suicides — were housed in a separate annexe connected to the main building by a special corridor which was always, of course, kept locked. Contact with the other blocks and with the women's wards, which were next to ours, was strictly forbidden.

The Recreation Room, or rather the small hall, for there was another, larger hall downstairs, was usually opened at eleven o'clock, and I went there in order to forget my bitter thoughts and have a breath of fresh air. They said that in the Recreation Room the windows were open all night but when I arrived I found the Suicides already in occupation.

In the Recreation Room people amused themselves as best they could, but generally in the same ways as they did in the ward — they played dominoes or draughts, the only difference being that here there were tables. Max came up to me with a box of draughts.

"Let's have a game," he suggested.

I declined the offer. I used to play when I was a boy but now I was not in the mood. Max and Rolf occupied one of the small tables and immediately a crowd formed round them. It seemed they were very strong players, second only to Krivin and Alyosha, the local champions.

Robert acted as referee, which meant forcing the audience back from the players and setting up a line of chairs as a barrier. It was a job which required not only strength but a loud voice, and this was why he was always hoarse. And I thought it was because he had a cold. Just as loudly he commented on the match, which sounded particularly funny because he could not pronounce his 'r's. Also he was proud of his position and looked like a tom cat who had recently received an important promotion.

Next to me stood a man I had noticed in the canteen. Tall and with a pipe clenched in his teeth, his yellow, bristly face and bloodshot eyes betraying an alcoholic. He had a prickly, disagreeable look about him and later Rolf introduced me. He was Ravich, an engineer, and I had guessed right: he suffered from that intensely Russian form of addiction to the bottle. One day he had stuck his head in a noose but somebody got to him in time, and they brought him here. I noticed that his hands trembled. Ravich hung around for a while and then left, probably went back to his ward.

I had no interest in the draughts either, and moved away. Leaning against the piano by the window I stood and smoked. From beyond the forest a cloud quickly appeared, huge and arched like the back of a giant bear. It was going to rain, yet I thought how wonderful it would be to be out in the woods. Why did I think about that now? Perhaps because the clouds lifted and the sun came out. After all, it was spring, late April. I looked at the sun and the blossoming trees and flowers whose scents couldn't reach me here through the double safety glass of the windows.

I had always been sensitive to nature. To get away

from the noise and bustle all around us I had always been ready to live in the woods and never go home. I could do without the town completely. When my mother was alive she said I spent more time in the woods than at home. Often — we lived at Izmailovo, the area almost outside town — I would spend the night in a haystack or on the ground under a tree. Now, staring out at the flowers and the sky which seemed to be almost parading their charms, I was vividly aware that I had been put in a cage, prevented from enjoying nature, from breathing the fresh air. I felt the unhappiest of people on this earth. Even the toughest man has these moments of desolation.

My gloomy thoughts were interrupted by the loud rendition of some jazz tune. I recognized "Chattanooga Choo Choo Train."

"You an American?" The *jazzman* stopped singing and stared at me.

I nodded.

"Well, I'm in here for jazz... I love jazz but my neighbours wouldn't let me sing it. I've tried to kill myself three times..."

He smiled happily and launched into "Pardon me, boy..."

I stared after the jazz-loving would-be suicide. At last he's happy because nobody here stops him 'singing' jazz!

From two to four was the Americans' exercise time. They issued us with quilted jackets, lined us up and let us out into the yard under the supervision of the orderly, Rakoff.

"No talking! Get a move on, scum!" he yelled, brandishing his club. Occasionally he speeded someone on with a thwack of his truncheon.

The Suicides were already out in the yard and started up a game of football with the Americans. There was no ball, just somebody's old boot. The game soon turned into a fight between the criminals from both wards against the Americans and Suicides. At first, the odds were in the criminals' favour — there were thirteen of them in the Suicides ward. The orderlies pretended to see nothing. But as soon as the Americans and Suicides got them into a corner, the orderlies rushed in using their clubs to beat up the Americans. I took no part in the game nor in the fight but stood by the railing. Not far away Alyosha squatted on the ground sketching. Up came a shortish man, his right arm missing up to the elbow.

"You a suicide?" he asked.

"No, an American," I replied gloomily.

"Well, I'm a suicide. Name's Nikita. What are you in for?"

"Oh, well, it's a long story..."

"Well, I told the officer at the draft board when he asked me whether I wanted to serve in the army, 'bugger off with your army!' Still, they took me in all the same and the very first day they stuck me in the cooler for a month. When I got out they sent some of us to a collective farm to cut timber and I gashed my arm with an axe.

44

Lost two litres of blood and nearly died, I did. They couldn't save the arm but it did get me out of the army..."

That night I dreamed heavily. Old Dementich, who was on ward duty, said I even cried out in my sleep. I dreamed I was in a forest. At first I was driving through in a car. Then I stopped it. The area was quite strange to me, the atmosphere somehow stifling. The forest was marvellously spacious, grotesque and romantic and it was as hot as in a Turkish bath. Leaving the car, I walked till I came to a house. The first thing I noticed was a terrace like an empty aquarium, and through the windows I could see strange, almost tropical blooms. I was choking for lack of breath: there was no breeze nor the slightest hope of one. At the same time, there was no sun either: everything was wreathed in clouds and it seemed from the room as though we were on the point of rain. But this was an illusion. If only there were some breeze, what a relief it would bring! Gasping I looked up at the treetops. Suddenly from behind a tree Lika emerged, slim, in the white dress and broad-brimmed hat she had worn that day. I dashed out of the house and rushed after her. I ran and ran until I found myself back in that strange, unfamiliar spot, flat as a billiard table. Beyond it deer grazed. They were purple in colour! I was amazed — where had they come from? Again I glimpsed Lika's dress. Wait, I shouted! But a man came up, took her hand and led her away.

I chased after them and saw that the man was Baliev. He was wearing a white hat and a red bow tie and he had that funny stick he had bought in an antique shop. They disappeared so quickly that I stood dumbfounded, at a loss what to do.

THIRD DAY

Next day was Sunday, but it was the same old routine. The Count, as ever, was into his singing from six o'clock onwards. A miserable breakfast and after that I sprawled on my bed, leafing through Max's dictionary.

"What's this book?" asked Dementich coming up to me. "Very odd, it looks. One half not like ours at all."

"This is an English-Russian dictionary. One word in Russian, and then this word in English."

"Hmmm... In English... I wonder how they manage to read all those scrawly hooks, those blinking heathens."

I went out into the corridor for a smoke, but before I had finished Vera Cabot appeared.

"Would you help me, Parkin?" she asked with devilish sweetness, taking me by the hand in front of a dozen people; it's a good thing Max wasn't there. He was called to the Suicides Ward to see Ravich.

"I have to make out a heading for a roster of night duties. Could you print one nicely for me?"

She took me into her office and pointed to a table

47

with a sheet of thick paper, pencils, pens, marking ink and all the other necessaries. Strange that she asked me when there was Alyosha, the artist. He could do it much better. Then I recalled that Alexei isn't interested in women, and Cabot knew it of course. I sat down and got on with the task. Back at school I used to be quite good at printing and things like that, and I was sure I could cope with a little thing like a heading.

Cabot was busy behind a screen.

"Would you like a cup of coffee?"

What a question! After drinking slops for two days, of course I'd like coffee.

I sipped the coffee and carried on printing her sign. The coffee seemed divine, although I noticed from the tin that it was just ordinary instant coffee, and I liked the freshly-ground stuff. I finished the sign, thanked her for the coffee and made my way towards the door.

"If you need anything, just come," she said in her velvety voice.

A woman who spelt trouble, what the hell did she want from me?

I left the office. Outside, waiting for me in the corridor, stood Max. Face pale, lips compressed.

"Well, how was it?" he asked.

"What do you mean?"

"Oh, come on, mate, you know. I'm just shattered that you managed it so quickly..."

"What on earth are you on about?"

"Well, didn't she, you know what I mean... well, that..."

"I was printing her a heading for a roster of night duties, at her request," I snapped and pushed past him.

"And that's all?" He dashed after me.

"That was all."

Immediately his face brightened, almost shone with happiness.

"You know, Vera and I... well, how can I put it? Frankly, I'm really gone on her. She's very young and, unfortunately for me, very beautiful. Everybody's after her, you see. And that, well it makes me furious."

I stopped and turned to face him.

"Whitley, get that idea out of your head. I don't get mixed up with my friends' women."

"Thanks, old man. I knew it. I knew you were okay."

We were called to the bath-house. Sunday was the Americans' bath day.

The bath-house was the same one where I took my shower that first evening. Under the supervision of the same pock-marked orderly we had our showers, seven at a time, as many as there were stalls. I was in one group with Max, Rolf, Robert, Leon, Alyosha and Dutschke. The next group was already there, waiting for us: engineer Ravich, Mike Kauffman, Vic Kotik, Hesse, Mayer and Marc Lerner. We soon finished and then we were turned over to three orderlies in a small room next to the showers. This was the barber's and here we were shaved and shorn. There were only three hair-clippers for thirty-eight men and all the Suicides had passed through that morning already. Naturally, they didn't rinse, clean or disinfect the clippers. It was the same with shaving. I got as embarrassed as every new inmate. When I came out of the shower I rubbed myself dry with the scrap of towel and got dressed. As I entered the barber's, one chair had just become vacant.

"Over here!" yelled an orderly.

I went over and intended to sit down.

"What the hell do you think you're doing? Stop that!"

I stared at him, completely puzzled.

"Get your trousers down!" he yelled again.

I glanced round at the others. Two orderlies were finishing shaving Max and Rolf, who sat imperturbably in the chairs. But I noticed that the orderlies were sniggering amongst themselves and I thought that mine was playing some joke. Again he yelled, this time more angrily:

"What the fuck are you farting around for? Get your trousers down when I say so!"

I did nothing of the sort; if this 'queer' starts bothering me, I'd smash his face in, I thought. But apparently it wasn't a joke; for the sake of hygiene they removed the pubic hair too. Max, hair cropped and face shaven, left. From the showers appeared Leon. He came up to the chair and dropped his trousers. The orderly began to shave him. There was nothing I could do. With the same razor he had used on at least a dozen others he shaved off my pubic hair and then, blowing the bristles off the blade, proceeded to shave my face. I tried not to think about it: I felt queasy enough as it was. The gruesome business over, I hurried from the room with relief.

6

I stood by the window watching the women walking in the yard. Viewed from above, in their drab quilted jackets and tatty headscarves they looked like grey crested birds. Suddenly from the ward came a piercing scream. People rushed from all sides. At this time of the day the ward was usually empty except for the cleaners. It turned out that some girl, hired only recently, had ignored the others' warning to lock herself in while she was cleaning. Now she lay spreadeagled on the floor in the middle of the room, half choked, her face blue and eyes rolled upwards. Her dress was up around her chin and her full, plump body trembled convulsively. Flattened against the wall behind the door was the Prophet, the same man who had attacked Leon yesterday at breakfast, puny and bald, with yellow skin stretched tight over his skull. He was breathing hard, his trousers down around his ankles and spittle drooling from his mouth.

Max and Rolf wanted to tear into him right there and then, but I stopped them. What's the point of beating up a miserable creature like him? He ought to be isolated. Dr Petters rushed into the ward, accompanied by Rakoff wielding his club. When he saw the orderly, the Prophet began to shudder and covered his head with his hands. In front of us all Rakoff hit him over the head with his club, pulled him out of the corner by his feet and dragged him off down the corridor.

Two older nurses turned up and helped the girl to her feet. Slowly she came round but was still shocked. Max and Rolf told me the Prophet was a very dangerous character — a sex maniac and a killer. That very first evening I had been struck by his vicious, contorted face.

He painted his cheeks with rouge he had hidden away somewhere. His skin hung down in flabby folds although he was not yet forty, but his most striking feature was that he was always smiling, baring black rotten teeth. Max told me he had been living with his wife and her old mother, whom he had regularly raped at knife point. He was not just a sex maniac — he even had his theories. He used to justify his excesses to his victims with religious arguments. In the end he set fire to his apartment after locking in it the victims of his sick passion. After that they brought him here. He used to write love letters to all the nurses and cleaners, would fly into jealous rages and pinched the behind of every woman, even the old ones.

"Why do they keep that lunatic in with us? He ought to be locked up in a cage," I commented violently.

"I asked Loza the same thing. He said: 'if he kills some Jewboy, or a couple of Germans, he is not responsible, after all, he is crazy, isn't he?' and just laughed," said Max. "But he was a bit drunk then."

"A drunken man speaks a sober mind. He is a bastard," said Rolf. "He incites the criminals and the orderlies against the Jews and the Germans."

"Against the politicals too. Krivin is constantly being beaten up by the criminals and the orderlies," Max swore rudely.

52

Grigory Krivin, the Marxist, came up to talk to me. He looked haggard from loss of weight and *treatment*. Like old Dementich said, he was almost translucent. He offered me his hand — so thin it was more like a chicken's claw — but his eyes shone with life and intelligence.

"Did you want to get out to the West, too?" he asked.

"No".

"I'm here for Marxism." He smiled sadly. "I would never have believed it if somebody had told me it was possible in a workers' and peasants' state based on Marx's teaching."

"Forgive the question, but how many days have you been in here?"

"Days?" he pondered. "I've never really worked it out, but let's see — it'll be one year, six months and four days..."

He was about to say something else when he was called away to the Treatment Room.

For all his outward alertness he was clearly a broken man. I learned later that he had twice tried to commit suicide and the orderlies had been instructed to keep him under special surveillance. *Special surveillance* meant that they, and Rakoff in particular, used to beat him up whenever they could. Later I was to see him in his black spells of hypochondria, when his skin went pale yellow and he trembled as though from the cold, although it was warm in our ward. In his lucid periods Grigory was quiet and talked little, using every opportunity to write something out of sight of the doctors and orderlies. After the fight between the criminals and the Americans in the yard and the following attack on the Americans by the orderlies and after what Max and Rolf had told

53

me, I realized that the orderlies and the criminals had been skilfully directed by Loza, the head of our department.

At five o'clock they brought in another lad by the name of Ustinov. He was Russian.

"You tried to get out to the West, too?" asked Max sarcastically.

"I didn't try, I was there."

"If you mean you fled there, you can cut out your fucking lies. If you'd done that, you'd be in prison by now. We only get people here who want to get out."

"And I tell you I've been in the West," Ustinov insisted.

"Are you trying to say you're a real American? Hi, how do you do, Mr Ustinov! But why've you got a Russian peasant face then?"

We laughed.

"I'm not American, I'm Russian, from Voronezh," said Ustinov, heedless of Max's mockery.

"We can see that."

"Well, I was working in America as a driver for a trade mission and got married to an American girl. They gave me permission. Then she suddenly left me for an American and I decided to come back. Things were okay at first, then I began telling my friends and neighbours how I had worked as a mechanic at a factory for a year and made enough to live on for two years without working and still come back here with some money. So they pulled me in and warned me to stop telling stories like that. Anyway I told them to go to hell. It was true, after all, so why the hell should I conceal it. Then I talked a lot more, just to spite them and they brought me here."

"Well, now it's all clear," Max nodded.

"What, you don't believe me?" shouted Ustinov, offended now. "I swear to you it's the honest truth! I worked a year, lived on my earnings for two and still came back with money in my pocket..."

"Oh yes, we believe you, we believe you. There's no need to swear." Rolf interrupted him. "I was just thinking, though, either you're a real loony or just stupid." He went up to Ustinov and tapped him on the forehead with his fingers. "Gets to America, comes back of his own free will and then goes around telling everybody what a paradise it is over there. Well, lads, it looks as though we have a real loony in the ward at last."

We all burst out laughing, but Ustinov, who evidently had no sense of humour whatsoever, was mortally offended and raged at the dwarf.

"You shut up, runt!"

"I'm not a runt, I'm a tall dwarf," drawled Robert with great dignity.

"Get away, there's no such thing as a tall dwarf."

"You don't know anything, Ustinov. You're just an ignorant fool. In Italy the average height of a man is one metre fifty-five centimetres; I read that in an Italian encyclopaedia. My height is one metre fifteen centimetres. Dwarfs' height is not above one metre. In Africa to this very day there is still a tribe of pygmies not above one metre in height. They would consider me a giant."

Ustinov stood gaping, silenced by Robert's arguments.

That evening everyone gathered in the Recreation Room for the American Ward's chess championship. At a table sat our two Grand Masters — Alyosha and Grigory Krivin — and around them crowded their audience, patients and even doctors and orderlies. Robert, as always, acted as referee. I watched for a while and then decided to go back to the ward. I felt sick at heart, in no mood for such entertainments, and since yesterday had been suffering from some queer headache centred at the back of my neck. Probably from some drugs they were mixing with the food.

I left the Recreation Room and decided to go along to the Treatment Room to get a tablet for my headache. I opened the door and saw what I had no desire to see. On the couch lay Rolf, dressed only in his underpants and bending over him, her arms around his neck, was Vera Cabot. When he saw me, Rolf jumped from the couch in great confusion, but Cabot just smiled, not the least embarrassed.

"I'm sorry," I said, and stepped back.

"Come back, Boris. We were just having an examination, right, Rolf?" She gave a cynical laugh.

Rolf said nothing but began to dress.

"Did you want something?"

"I was looking for a pill for my headache. I'll come

back later," I mumbled.

"Don't go away, I'll give you a tablet." She came to the door and took me by the hand.

"I've changed my mind, lady; I don't want a tablet," I angrily thrust her away with my free hand and slammed the door.

At the Recreation Room the match was at its peak, and Alyosha was winning. After a while I noticed Rolf sidle in and merge with the crowd. He saw me. I was standing at the other end of the room right opposite him. He began to make his way across the room.

"Where's Whitley?" he asked quietly.

"His mother's come to see him. He's probably downstairs," I said, as though nothing had happened.

"Come over here, there's something I have to tell you. I wouldn't like you to think I started all that," he said when we were at a safe distance from the chess fans. "She called me in for an examination, told me to get undressed and then started in on me. You know, Bob, between ourselves, I agree she's got a good pair of legs and a terrific pussy, but she's also the biggest bitch ever. Nothing on her mind except men and clothes. I just don't know what's got into Max..."

My opinion exactly.

"You think it's just with me? She had a thing going with Vic Kotik, then with Dutschke, the whole ward knew about it, except Whitley, of course. Then she started making eyes at Krivin, but he told her to bugger off, so I'm not the first". He moved away and shortly after left the Recreation Room.

FOURTH AND FIFTH DAYS

Next morning I was called to the Treatment Room. Waiting for me were Dr Petters and Vera Cabot.

"I have to examine you, Parkin, and ask you some questions," said Petters. "The Commission will be seeing you after lunch."

They began by getting me to stand on a board with a sliding rule to measure my height.

"Right, one metre eighty, Vera. Jot it down. Now, stand on the scales, please. Seventy-five kilograms. Sit down here and cross your legs."

I sat down and did what she asked. She looked at me, bent over and tapped me smartly on the knee cap with a little hammer. My leg jerked very slightly.

"Your nerves are good," said Petters nastily and tapped me again on the knee with her hammer.

She asked me to shut my eyes and touched my hand with a sort of metal spatula, then a sharp scalpel and then with the blunt handle of some instrument. Each time I correctly named the sort of thing she was using.

After that she sat down and wrote up her notes, occasionally tossing a Latin name at Cabot.

"You're interested in women, of course?" she suddenly asked, continuing to write.

I was about to answer when the telephone rang. Dr
Petters picked up the receiver, listened and said nothing
except for the occasional 'yes' and 'no'. She replaced
the receiver and stood up with an anxious look.

"Carry on here, Vera. I've got to go and receive a new
patient. You know what we need to find out."

She left, and I was all alone with Cabot. She looked
at me provocatively, her cheeks flaming and making her
still more attractive.

"Let's carry on, Boris. Right. Now are you interested
in sex, I mean, women?"

"Why, what's it to you?"

"We have to know that in order to draw up a psycho-
logical report on you for the Commission. Are you
interested in women older than you? If you do, how
much older? And if not, how much younger? Or do you
prefer women of your own age?"

She was so self-assured I had to say something:

"I don't know. I never ask them for their birth certi-
ficate before getting them into bed".

"Are you refusing to answer my questions? After all,
you can tell roughly how old a woman is?" she persisted,
trying to get some sort of dialogue going. "And another
thing, do you prefer dominant women, or do you like to
be the boss yourself?"

"Yea, I like dominant women like you. How about it
then, right here, you seem to manage the rest of the
ward..."

I had called her bluff.

"What? Get out of here, get out!" she yelled, running to the door.

Late that afternoon I was suddenly summoned to Loza, head of the Seventh Department. Must be because of that bitch. This was the first time we'd met; for some reason he was not on the Commission at 2.00 p.m. Determined to give vague answers to all questions and reveal nothing about myself I turned the massive handle of the door to his office and came suddenly face to face with Gipsy. I have already mentioned that he controlled the criminals in the Suicides Ward. He was taking instructions, I decided in my mind. I let him pass without a word.

Beneath a group of portraits, in a large office furnished with surprising luxury, sat a plump man in his mid-fifties with thick lips and a face as pink as a piglet's. His cold eyes slithered over me and his neatly trimmed silver moustache contorted into a cunning smile. He did not ask me to sit down, so I stood and examined his fat legs, thrust out from under the table and clad in silk socks and excellent soft leather shoes of foreign make.

"Why did you play the fool before the Commission today, Parkin?" he began. "I look at you and I see a completely healthy fellow, intelligent enough not to be involved in politics. But some of the things you get up to... Well, you can tell me what the trouble is. What was all that business with your friend? Some private

60

score to settle? Some squabble over a woman? Come on... Tell me in confidence. I won't tell anyone else. It was an expensive house and your friend has an important job and he's got the highest connections. So what was it all about? Why did you do it?"

"I just didn't like his ugly mug."

"That's what you told the Commission, and it didn't go down in your favour. So you can give up that attitude, Parkin. And another thing — why do you go around always pretending to be a hooligan, some sort of rough-neck? You'd better alter your ways. And what were you thinking of talking to Cabot like that when she was examining you? Why did you scare her like that? She's terrified of you now..."

"Jesus fucking Christ, me, terrified Cabot... Could anybody terrify her?"

"Shut up! Don't talk to me like that. What are you trying to achieve? Do you want to get yourself in a strait-jacket, locked up in the Violent Wing?" He stared at me with bulging eyes.

"Look, you graduate from university, and yet you go off and work as a driver. Why? Do you want to spend your entire life mixing with the working class, that drunken lot?"

A nasty smile creased his thick lips.

"Your father was an important journalist, your mother was a doctor and you have a first-class educa-tion — so what is all this performance for? Now, I'll tell you bluntly, the Commission couldn't agree about you. You made a very unfavourable impression on them and they've decided to keep you here for the time being. We won't be giving you any treatment — yet. Not until the first time you start breaking the rules. Do you get

61

me? Now then, let's talk seriously. I want you to tell me everything, right from the start. First of all, what made you go off and become a driver?"

"I like to travel. I told them that on the Commission."

"Cut it out, I don't believe you. If you like to travel, there's your holidays. Travel as much as you want then; nobody's stopping you. Take a car or a plane as befits a man of your position."

"It's not the same thing, holidays. I like to travel all the time. Working as a driver I get to see different people, different places. I couldn't work in an office from nine to six."

"If you insist on that tack, you can go. I can see you'll come to a bad end."

They left me there for *observation* until the next Commission with the diagnosis 'under-estimation of his own talents as a result of latent schizophrenia, also revealed in the form of sudden outbursts of temper.' Max got this from Vera Cabot. 'Under-estimation of his own talents' referred to my working as a driver, and the 'outbursts of temper' to the incident of Baliev's house. If it hadn't been for that damned house, of course, they wouldn't have held me here for the driving thing, but since I was here, that was something the doctors simply could not understand. Not that I could blame them. Nobody would understand except my mother and Lika, and my mother was no longer there. Nor was Lika.

My university friends were all working for news-papers, publishing houses or for television. The least successful of them were teaching at schools in Moscow. When they learned that I had quit the Art History Institute for no apparent reason, they gradually dropped me, stopped asking me to their parties. Anyway, I didn't need them. My friends here, Max and Rolf, did not understand me either. Especially Max.

"They're keeping you here," said Max. "Look, Bob, when you were telling us about Baliev, you said you'd done it because of some girl. We can understand that, and we can understand you punching your boss, but we can't understand what the hell you're doing in a working man's job with your qualifications. Just think why they're keeping you here — it's not because you flatten-ed his house. They could get compensation for that out of you through the court. Of course, they picked you up after he rang the police, but they'd have let you go the next day if it hadn't been for that. You must agree. See, you do agree! We tell you frankly we don't con-sider you a loony, but the others did when they heard about it..."

Max was just like Loza — why, why, why had I joined the working class? Everybody wants to know that. They all want to shove their noses into my private life.

"Okay, I'll tell you, if that's what interests you." I looked at them and thought what the hell, they won't understand. "Well, I'd been taking a cool look at the world for quite a while and I found nothing good in it. Does that seem strange to you? I want to be a free man, not a careerist. I'm not a pushing type, I'm not ambitious, I just want to get on with my own life in my own little corner of the world. Tell me, what sort of history of art or philosophy can we have when we're right back in the Dark Ages? I'll give you an example. I've just wasted seven fucking years — all those useless diplomas. The miserable bit of knowledge they drummed into me at university I could have read up for myself with better effect. I'm sorry now I didn't study engineering or medicine; those are useful professions, but now it's too late. Ten years ago, by the way, I used to think like you do. My philosophy is not to fight anybody or anything; that's a sheer waste of time and energy. I don't need any of that stuff — career, high life — I just want to live. And as for education, well, I got my real education by myself, and that's still with me."

"Yes," sighed Rolf, "it's interesting, what you say. I agree absolutely."

7

"Seeing as how you're staying, Bob, you ought to join our Loonies Club and the American Club straight away," Max told me as we were getting ready for bed.

"What are they?" I was curious.

"The Loonies Club — that's our trade union. It defends your interests with the administration, so that if anything happens to you and you're a member, the Loonies Club takes some action. First of all, your case is made known outside the hospital. Second, if you're

punished unjustly, our members petition the doctors
for your release, and if that doesn't work they help in
every way they can. For instance, we've got orderlies
on our side in the Violent Wing. Things like that. The
American Club is a purely philanthropic enterprise.
We use the monthly contributions to buy cigarettes,
milk, fruit juice and things like that. We also use the
money to bribe orderlies in special cases and to finance
special occasions like birthday parties. The Loonies Club
contribution is one rouble, ours is two. If you don't
have any money, you can give some article instead. The
system's simple — the American Club sells the articles
to the criminals; they always have money and they'll
buy anything. They sell them to people outside, through
their orderlies, but that's their business. The president
and founder of the Loonies Club is Ravich, the engineer
in the Suicides Ward. You remember him — the serious
chap with the pipe. He's got two assistants — Dutschke
and Vic Kotik. And the treasurer is Alyosha. I'm president of the American Club, my vice-president is Rolf,
and Robert is my treasurer."

"You couldn't have a better man than Ravich for
negotiating", Rolf said. "He's the official steward of the
Seventh Department, and Loza and the administration
listen to what he says because he's not a political and
he's not a Jew. The same with Alyosha, he's talented and
ordinary folk have a weakness towards talent. Dutschke
is a dentist and Loza himself goes to him, for all that
he's a German."

"Okay, I'm in," I agreed. "I don't have any money
with me — they took it all away when they brought me
in — but if you like I can give you a notebook. It's
foreign-made, real leather binding. There's just one page
used, but I can tear it out so nobody will notice." I took

the book from my jacket pocket and offered it to Max.

"Ah, now this is better than money. I'll get at least ten roubles out of the Count for this." He took the book and stuck it in his pocket.

"Okay, you're a member of both clubs — bar a few small formalities. We'd better take you along to Ravich and Dutschke."

Leon, who had been sitting quietly on the next bed, suddenly began rummaging in his pockets.

"Here, Bob," he held out a home-made twenty-five rouble banknote. "I'll give you this for petty expenses. I just have to sign it." He scrawled his signature and offered me the note.

Max winked at me.

"Thanks, Leon, you've really helped me out." Poor chap, I took the 'note' from him and put it in my pocket.

Next morning, in a matter of ten minutes, I was admitted to the two organizations and after breakfast the members of the American Club and the Loonies Club got together to celebrate both my admission and Leon's birthday.

Rolf and Robert poured each member a small glass of surgical spirit diluted with water, stolen from a laboratory by the criminals and sold to us, and we all clinked glasses. Then Leon was presented with a huge sandwich spread with real butter and mashed aubergine and bristling with thirty-one flaming matches, one for each year of Leon's life. Leon loved the sandwich, and the butter, and the aubergine, and the flaming matches; he laughed and clapped his hands in delight. Rolf showed him how to blow out the matches, and comically Leon inflated his cheeks and got them all out with one blow. Everyone applauded and congratulated him.

Following this the American Ward was the scene of another event. Our dormitory was invaded by the Suicides, and even doctors and nurses came, too, for today Alyosha was to begin modelling a statue of Rolf. From the beginning of his admission he had been asking the administration for permission and that morning Loza had come along and said he could get on with it — as 'occupational therapy'. Everyone was delighted. Alyosha walked around looking very solemn: he had got everything he needed for the job stored up in the nurses' room, and now he staggered into the ward, all red in the face from the weight of a box containing his clay and tools. A full-length statue was out of the question: this would be a smaller figure on a stand. The administration wouldn't let Alyosha tackle anything larger, and anyway it would have been very inconvenient in a hospital ward. Loza had also insisted that the figure should represent a sportsman and, once completed, would become the hospital's property. Alyosha agreed to any condition just for the chance to sculpt again. Today, right after breakfast, he got down to the job, breaking off reluctantly only for mealtimes or when Rolf was called away. He had chosen Rolf for his muscular physique. Rolf had at first refused to pose because, as he had crudely put it, he couldn't stomach that bloody queer. Finally Max had talked him round, and now he stood in his underpants in the centre of the room posing as a basketball player. Around him, two or three to a bed, sat the audience. The most comical sight was Robert in Leon's lap. Robert, in keeping with his referee status, maintained order.

From time to time the nurses looked in, and old Dementich sat on my bed sighing. Rakoff, very curious, also poked his head in but he knew Loza had given permission and he could see that good order was being maintained. There was no scope for his bullying here.

By evening Alyosha had transformed the wire carcass into something vaguely human, although as yet there was nothing of Rolf in it. When he knocked off for the day everyone came up in turn to inspect the work, and as a service to 'the artist', as he now called him, Robert fetched a broom and began to sweep up around the figure.

Our criminals — the Count, Musa and Simon — also came up to have a look. The Count sneered:

"Hey, Kraut, is this you then?"

Musa and Simon sniggered. Rolf stepped up to the Count and hit him hard on the jaw. The Count fell to the floor and his mates piled into Rolf.

"Cool it!" bellowed Max.

The criminals re-grouped and backed towards the door. Rolf stood there, red, fists clenched.

"Cool it!" said Max, quieter now. "I warn you, Count, if any of your mob lifts a finger against anyone here, there'll be some ribs broken. Even if they send me to the Violent Wing for it. Get me?"

The Count got the message and as he knew Max he signalled to his mates to beat it. Deep down he was afraid of Max.

8

Out for our walk Max and Rolf drew me aside.

"On Sunday there's a football match on between the Americans and the Suicides. They've given us special permission because it's May Day — International Workers Day. As a matter of fact, it was the Loonies Club that got the permission out of them; Ravich, Dutschke, Vic Kotik and Alyosha have been working on the administration for the past two weeks. Point is, do you want to play?" Max said, eyes smiling.

"Where's it going to be held?"

"Well, here of course, in the yard. Where'd you think, in Lenin Stadium?" Rolf laughed.

I'd played for my faculty team at university, and the chance of really stretching my limbs was tempting. Despite my rotten mood, I agreed.

"The Suicides have got two strong players, Pyotr Dutschke, their captain, and Mike Kauffman. They've both played in professional matches, as forwards. I'll put you in the centre, along with me and Rolf. It that all right, can you cope?"

I nodded.

"Right, then, let's get down to some training."

From his jacket pocket he extracted a ball little bigger than a baby's head.

I felt much better after the training and by the time we went into the canteen I was so famished I could have eaten a horse. I mopped up my dish of porridge and today it seemed perfectly normal, quite edible and even tasty. Max didn't want his, so I ate that too, and Rolf — seeing me mop up both dishes so clean they didn't need washing — winked at Max.

On the way out of the canteen Max introduced me to Pyotr Dutschke, a dentist.

"Pete", he said holding out his hand and beaming a big smile.

I left them discussing the details of the match and returned to the ward. I saw Musa, the Tartar, his eyes more slanted than ever, standing on somebody's bed pissing a figure-eight design on the floor to the accompaniment of loud guffaws from the Count and his mates. Then he snatched Leon's doll away and tossed it to Simon. Leon, arms raised, ran after them, a tall ridiculous figure, begging them to give him his 'Ninochka' back. The Count egged them on.

Everybody was watching the scene in silence, scared of interfering and tangling with the Count. Max and Rolf were still away with Dutschke in the Suicides Ward and of our lot there was only Robert, clenching his tiny fists.

Just after me Alyosha entered the ward. At once he went up to the Count.

"Leave Leon alone! He's sick and defenceless".

The Count's face twisted into a grin. Suddenly he started to drop his trousers.

"Here, sculptor, how about modelling my prick?"

Alyosha flushed bright red. Neither the Count nor anyone else in the ward knew about Alyosha. Loza himself had issued instructions that Alyosha's sexual inclinations be kept a secret from the other patients. To them Alyosha was here as a drug addict, which was more or less the truth. Of course, a few trusted orderlies must have known about Alyosha from Loza. Max had learned about it from Vera Cabot, but the secret had gone no further than Rolf and me. Probably Alyosha himself did not realize we knew. Now he stood alone, face to face with the Count, and was at a loss at what to do.

The doll was now with Simon, I stepped up and hooked his feet from under him so that he toppled over onto a bed. I threw the doll to Leon. There was a silence. The Count advanced on me in the middle of the room.

"Fuck me. You're really looking for trouble, Yank."

I kicked him hard. He fell, but was on his feet again in an instant. Behind him were ranged the Tartar and Simon, ready to start fighting. Spread out, they drove Alyosha and me back into the corner. I knew they would be armed with knives. By himself the Count was no danger — he was a coward — but the Tartar and Simon together were real hard cases. But we were lucky; at that moment, fetched by the dwarf, Max, Rolf, Dutschke and Mike Kauffman entered the ward. The fight began. Vic Kotik, Mayer and Marc Lerner heard the noise and came in on our side. We soon got the upper hand. The Count, seeing they were outmatched, ordered his mates to 'cool it', but Musa continued to fight. We knocked him down. Simon was wearing a knuckleduster and we wrested it from him.

"Okay, Whitley, your mob wins this time," snarled the Count bending over to pick up the knuckleduster.

I stepped hard on his hand. Furious, he backed away

and he and his mates reluctantly and humiliated left the ward.

"The Count will never forgive you for this," remarked Max.

I shrugged. The incident brought me another friend, Leon. For days afterwards he followed me around like a shadow, looking at me with devoted doglike eyes and sometimes so intelligently that it gave me the creeps.

I lay on my bed, tormented by hunger. Obviously the effect of all that training. It's curious that people don't get bored eating every day. Hunger comes again and again, and without that eating would bore them — like everything else in life. Now, after just a few days I can see our main problem. The Americans' chief problem is how to stay fed and how to get enough sleep. We get woken up in the early hours by shouts, sometimes fights and all kinds of foolery from the criminals, feigning this or that illness, and we are constantly hungry. We are allowed one parcel of up to two kilograms a week. Of our lot only Max and Robert received parcels. Rolf and I had nobody. Robert got fruit and sweets from his midget girlfriend. These the dwarf loved. He was very kind-hearted and everything he got he willingly shared with us. Not only with us but with everyone he liked, and he liked Leon because he understood his suffering and now he respected Alyosha, because he was an artist.

Max barely touched the hospital food. His mother

doted on him and did everything she could to help. Through some intricate system of bribes she managed to visit her son three times a week instead of the one regular visit on Sundays, and she always brought a basket of the best produce available. Rolf told me she had exellent contacts. Even after Max was arrested, she held her top position. She continued to work with foreigners and travel abroad. Strange as it may seem, this was because somebody at the very top level remembered her husband's services to the State. Anyway, Max and Robert helped to feed us, as well as Leon and, for a time now, Alyosha.

From the corridor came a dreadful shriek. We rushed out in time to see Rakoff, club in hand, burst out of the toilets. He tore down the corridor like a rocket and disappeared through the staff door. We went into the toilets, fearing for Robert whom Rakoff had recently picked on. He had beaten him several times. But this time the victim was Grigory Krivin, our Marxist. Rakoff had picked on him for something and hit him over the head knocking him unconscious. We called Dr Petters and the nurses to help bring Krivin round. Soon he was lying in his bunk, head all bandaged.

SIXTH DAY

Next day Ravich called a meeting of the Loonies Club to discuss the matter. We argued and argued but came to no decision about Rakoff.

"We should call him in and warn him that if he touches Krivin again we'll complain to the administration," Dutschke said.

"The administration doesn't give a shit about Krivin. They put him up to it," Ravich replied.

I agreed with him absolutely.

"Yes, that won't help," said Alyosha. "The only language Rakoff understands is force."

"Alyosha's right," Rolf chimed in. "There's no point trying to re-educate a thug."

"Remember, he was pissed out of his mind," I said.

"I want to teach him a lesson this time," Max muttered darkly.

"I forbid anything of the sort, Whitley," warned Ravich strictly.

We respected Ravich: he carried a lot of weight among us. After that nobody had any more suggestions and the Loonies Club meeting ended.

That evening, after keeping well away all day, Rakoff suddenly entered our ward. We sat on a bed playing cards and studiously ignored him, but all the others scattered like disturbed bedbugs. They feared Rakoff, and this thug well knew it. From the doorway he announced:

"Don't be afraid, lads. I'm in a good mood today."

He came straight up to our bed: for the first time he was without his club and seemed to be quite sober.

"Hey, Whitley," it was the first time he had addressed him as anything but 'Yank'. "I hear your ma works with foreigners and..."

"Well, so what?" Max cut in brusquely.

"Ask your ma to get me a bottle of whisky. She must have some foreign currency coupons. I'll give you a quarter." From his pocket he extracted a twenty-five rouble note and waved it.

We looked at one another.

"I'll think about it, Rakoff, now piss off..."

"What's the matter with you? This is straight up".

"Pisss offf... Get me?" Max's eyes flashed.

"Okay... okay... I'm off".

9

Every day somebody new was admitted, but nobody was discharged. We got three more: another criminal, a young Jewish boy who was studying at the Conservatoire and an old man. The student, a violinist, was called Sasha Feldman. The old man was a very strange type — he had an inspired sort of face and long, biblical hair. It could have been the head of Christ, but crazed with fear.

"Who is he?" we asked Dementich.

"He is a collective farm worker and before that he was a peasant." Dementich clearly divided these two categories.

Dementich told us later that he had quit his collective farm and run off into the wood. There he had dug himself an underground shelter in which he had lived for three months, hence the long hair. They had tracked him down with dogs and brought him straight here.

"Just think, friends, tracking him with dogs! And him going off to live underground."

We felt as ashamed as though it were us that had hunted the man down; we stood and gazed down at him on the floor, still bound, his eyes fixed unseeing on some distant horizon.

"Ask him if he wants some milk or an apple, Robert."

Max rummaged in his pocket for the American Club's account book.

But Christ from the collective farm wanted only one thing — to be left in peace.

On the same day came the incident with Sasha Feldman. We were standing in the corridor, smoking, when loud yells started coming from the ward. I was about to rush in when Max grabbed me by the sleeve.

"Don't go in, there's nothing you can do. They're force-feeding Sasha. He's gone on hunger-strike and Loza's ordered him to be force-fed."

"But why has he gone on hunger-strike?"

"Well, first of all for bringing him here and secondly because Rakoff called him publicly a 'bloody Yid'. Sasha went straight to Petters and demanded Rakoff's dismissal."

"Why did they bring him here, anyway?"

"He slapped the colonel across the face at a military training session in front of the whole class for saying that during the war Jews found themselves nice, safe, cushy jobs in the rear. He said that those who were in the army were cowards."

"Look, can't we do something? I can't stand hearing him scream like that..."

"What can we do? You can't fight six orderlies at once, although we could perhaps try talking to him and persuading him to give up this hunger-strike business?"

Soon the screams stopped and I went into the ward. Sasha was lying bound, exhausted and deathly pale. I'd taken an immediate liking to him when they brought him in; I liked his open frank look. He was only twenty-two, wore glasses and had strong Semitic features. I sat down on his bed.

"Sasha, when we get out of here come along to the garage and I'll teach you to drive."

"I don't know. Perhaps I'll come," he said weakly. "But when will that be?"

"Soon, Sasha, I'm sure. Quite soon."

"They'll let you out. They brought you in for fighting with the police, they told me..."

77

"It's not quite how it was, but more or less."

"After the holiday they'll let you out, but not me. They don't forgive our sort."

"Sasha," I laid my hand on his shoulder, "... listen, maybe all this isn't necessary. What's the point of starving yourself to death? You'll not change their minds but you could ruin your health. See, they force-feed you anyway."

"I don't know, perhaps you're right. How I hate them!" His face contracted with such pain that it went right to my heart.

"Look, Sasha, you must live to spite them. That's what you've got to do. Don't get worked up over scum like Rakoff. Who is he, anyway?"

Sasha's face lit up with a brief smile.

"All right, I'll think it over. But, forgive me Boris, now I'd like to sleep."

He fell asleep, exhausted morally and physically, of injections of aminazine and some other strong drugs. I stared at him with bitter feeling.

Our Loonies Club swung into action. Ravich, Alyosha and Rolf presented Loza with our petition insisting that Sasha be untied. And when that didn't have any effect we staged a demonstration in the canteen. We — eighteen Americans at three tables, led by Max, Pete Dutschke, Vic Kotik and Mike Kauffman — and twelve Suicides at another two tables — pushed aside our plates at a signal from Ravich and began to hammer on the table

78

with our spoons. The loonies and the criminals perked up at the chance of some fun and supported us. Not all of them refused their food, but they all hammered away enthusiastically. The orderlies took fright and summoned the doctors. In came Loza with Petters and Vera Cabot. Ravich got to his feet and repeated our demand that Sasha be untied.

"All right! All right!" shouted Loza through the din. "We'll discuss it. Just stop hammering and eat your food..."

"We want Sasha! We want Sasha!"we chorused in reply.

"Calm down! Stop it! Friends, comrades..." Loza tried to make himself heard above the din.

"We're no friends or comrades of yours!"somebody yelled.

"Fuck off... boss", shouted Gipsy. "We want the musician!"

Everyone yelled, stamped their feet and hammered on the tables. Two schizos jumped on a table and tipped soup on their heads. The orderlies dragged them off.

Incapable of quelling the din, the administration cleared off and a few minutes later old Dementich brought in Sasha, pale and very weak on his pins. We applauded him, and we applauded ourselves because we had won a victory. From now on there were six at our table — the sixth was Sasha Feldman.

Today was a really crazy day. After tea at five nobody went along to the Recreation Room. We all hung around the ward to watch Musa give Simon a new tattoo on his behind in honour of the holiday. The Tartar had all the tools and materials, an entire *laboratory* which he kept hidden in Simon's mattress. Fascinated, we watched him work — all except for Robert who kept watch by the door to warn if an orderly or a doctor showed up.

Today, at 2.00 p.m., there was another incident. As usual they let us out for our walk, but because of some confusion they had not yet cleared the yard of the women from the neighbouring block. The women all looked alike: they were dressed in terrible grey overalls and over these the same sort of quilted jackets as the men. Shod in ugly, shapeless boots they were pale and almost all dishevelled and uncombed, but still Musa and Simon made a beeline for them. Behind them raced Gipsy and his gang, closely followed by the rest of us. It was the first time we were operating in concert with the criminals. That's what women meant to us. The female orderlies tried to drive us back.

"Clear off! Get away!" they shouted, attempting to clear a path and hustle their charges back into their block.

But that's not how things worked out.

"Fuck off, you old bitch! Let's get a feel at the girls!" roared Gipsy.

Our combined efforts burst the chain of orderlies, ours and theirs. First to reach the women was our Tartar, Musa, who clutched the fattest of them, squeezing and kneading her breasts and buttocks and trying to ruck her skirt up at the back. The woman, far from resisting, squealed with delight and hugged Musa back. Seeing their friend's success, the other women rushed to join us. A slim dark-haired girl latched on to me and began kissing and hugging.

"Hey, gorgeous, what about a fuck?"

"Now? Where?"

"In the toilet, it's open, quick."

At this moment she was hauled away by a large female orderly.

"You old cow, you stinking old bitch! Get your hands off me!" yelled my girl.

Six more orderlies rushed to the assistance and a real fight began. The orderlies were all armed with clubs and gave us a hell of a beating.

Musa was fighting like a tiger against half a dozen orderlies who were trying to pull him away from his woman. She cursed them roundly and would not be parted from the Tartar. Then one of the orderlies clubbed him to the ground and they dragged him off to the far corner of the yard where the other orderlies, arms linked, had us penned in. Now it was easy to drive the women back into their block.

Only three people took no part in the assault on the women: Alyosha, Krivin, a serious chap, who was sickened by such behaviour, and the Count, who will always do the exact opposite to Gipsy, whom he hated. They had always been mortal enemies and they fought unceasingly for power over the criminals. The Count spat scornfully as his mate, Musa, his head bleeding, was borne past him on a stretcher.

Once the door to the women's block was shut, Dr Petters came out into the yard and told us we were deprived of our walk for this breech of order. We were driven back into our block, but nobody complained particularly. After all, a bit of excitement had relieved our boredom. Back in the ward all talk still centred around women.

"The food's shit and they won't even let you look at a woman," complained Vic Kotik to Hesse and Mayer.

"You're quite right," Ustinov backed him.

"Which would you rather have — a good steak or a nice pussy?" asked Mayer.

"Probably a steak."

"But I've seen women only in the movies," complained a youth who had recently been moved to us from the chronics' department. It turned out that of his 19 years he had spent 8 in various hospitals.

"I'd like a woman, one with a good white arse on her," sighed Simon.

"I wouldn't mind having a bash at that Loza. He's got an arse better than any woman's," said the Count, who had got over his mate's treacherous defection.

Talk of the devil! Just then Loza came in and began to lecture us on our conduct. He was ashamed of us, he said, for attacking the women like that.

"And when was the last time you got laid, boss?" called out Simon.

"Hey, boss. You've got a nice soft arse. You'll do me in place of a bird," the Count began to advance on Loza.

Loza went pale, turned and dashed out of the ward. A few minutes later eight orderlies came in. In complete silence they grabbed Simon and the Count and hauled them off to the Treatment Room for an injection. Both shouted and struggled furiously and Simon yelled the block down.

That night I could not sleep. I was pursued by nightmares: at one moment I was being dragged away, resisting desperately, at the next tied to my bed and injected
with a huge needle. Then, an axe was poised above my
head, somebody's blood dripping from the blade. Writhing, I tore myself loose and fled — right into the path of
a herd of sad-eyed horses.

I woke up soaked with sweat. Lying in my bed, I had
a sudden clear vision of Lika.

10

In the beginning there were two of us after her — Baliev
and I. We had studied at the philosophy department
together: Baliev graduated, but in the third year, a year
before my diploma, I switched over to history. We had
never been friends; I can't stomach snobs and social
climbers and he was both, and as it later transpired he
was a coward and a bastard as well. He was always
smartly dressed, though nobody knew where he got the
money from.

He had very decent parents but they were ordinary
working class people and had no money to spare. I
should add that he was ashamed of his parents and looked for friends among people whose parents held some
prominent position. That was why he made up to me,
because of my father, but I kept him away from my
home. It's curious that, although he bought only foreign
clothes, he used to turn up at university dressed in some

old, well-worn suit because, as he explained, he didn't want to stand out from 'those mongrels'. It was rumoured that he was involved with older women, actresses, general's wives — women like that — and was always careful to conceal his social origins from them. Again, because of his parents, he never asked his women or his friends (if he ever had any) home. His parents lived in a basement flat in a working class area. As you can gather, Baliev was an utter nonentity, and yet he was as vain as a woman about his appearance. He would spend hours in front of a mirror and moan for weeks about a pimple on his face. Somehow he managed to struggle through the philosophy course, graduated and — through a woman — landed a job on the editorial staff of a magazine. Once he became an editor, he blossomed out, he began openly wearing expensive foreign suits, got hold of bottles of French cognac, played the horses and within a couple of years was travelling abroad.

I would probably never have run into him again if it had not been entirely by chance. As a result of steady boozing he developed an ulcer, as well as some nervous disorder and God knows what, and ended up in front of my mother on the operating table. She fixed him up and within a couple of months he was as right as rain. So he decided he ought to come round and thank my mother. He turned up with a girl.

"My name is Lika," she said.

"Hello," I mumbled, glancing at her briefly and without getting up.

"Please, sit down, do!" my mother insisted. By then my father was no longer alive.

I was immediately taken by her face, delicate, open and sad. I well remember thinking at the time: beauty is almost always sad. I've yet to meet a happy beauty. I sat around like a stone and took no part in the conversation for I felt that, since becoming a lorry driver, I had lost any attraction for women of my own circle. So I decided to be brusque with her right from the start. As we were on the point of eating Lika asked if she might go and wash her hands, and my mother took her off to the bathroom. As soon as they were out of the room Baliev whispered to me:

"A ballerina from Leningrad. I picked her up at a party. Not bad, is she? Real class!"

"Are you having it off with her?" I asked him.

If so, that avenue would be blocked straight away, but in my heart I desperately hoped she was still free.

"I only met her yesterday, but she's really gone on me!" he gestured emphatically.

You shit, I thought. After supper Baliev asked me to give them a lift home. I knew that Lika lived a long way off, with friends near the new university building. From our flat in Izmailovo to Baliev's place was about a twenty-minute drive and soon I was pulling to a stop in front of his house.

"Here we are then..."

"Not this entrance, that one with the yellow door," he said.

I realized that, ashamed of his parents, this bastard must have rented another room in the same house.

"I've got a bottle of French cognac upstairs, Lika, how about coming in for a drink?" He turned to her, making it patently obvious that I was not invited.

"No, thanks. I've got a bit of a headache so I think I'll get an early night," she said with such directness that even the thick-skinned Baliev realized it was no use trying to talk her round.

"So you'll take the lady home, old man? Bye for now, kids!" he called, slamming the door.

We entered the university area in silence. She looked at her tiny gold watch and said:

"Perhaps you would be so kind as to show me something of Moscow?"

"Yes, of course, but I thought you weren't feeling well. You said you had a headache."

"I'm sorry, I just said that to get away from him."

"Ah, I understand."

We drove around the city for quite a while, generally in silence. My strategy was to play it very cool with her. I thought she was flirting with me, out of boredom, so I decided to find out what she was like before I made any move.

"Maybe we could go and have a drink somewhere?" she suggested.

I took her to a bar on Arbat Street and ordered some beer.

"Would you like another, or do you want to go home?" I asked with a refined politeness I hadn't thought I was capable of.

"Home..." she said drily.

It was late, really time to get her home. I had to be up early in the morning. We got into the car and were just about to drive off when I heard a stifled sob.

"What's the matter?"

"Tell me, why do you hate me so? What have I done?"

"Me?" I exclaimed, switching off the engine and turning to face her.

"Hate you? Quite the opposite."

"Yes, you hate me," she insisted, through her tears.

"You haven't even looked at me once..."

At that moment I was so conscious of her lips I could have kissed her on the spot, but I laughed instead and reached for her hands.

"Lika, you want to know the truth?"

"Yes, I do."

I stared into her beautiful, lively and at the same time sad face and felt that all my *tactics* weren't worth a damn.

"I love you. I fell in love with you at first sight — like an idiot, like a mere boy. I thought at first you must be Baliev's girlfriend and when I realized you were unattached I said to myself: whatever would she want with me?"

She smelled faintly of perfume but this could not conceal her own fresh, spicy fragrance. And that's how I came to know her. Shortly after that we began to live together, shuttling back and forth between two houses. Either I was with her in Leningrad (she had her own apartment) or she came to stay with mother and me. And then one day she gave me the silver ring with the inscription: "To Boris Henry James from Lika". She bestowed this surname on me because I usually had one of his books in my pocket: I had a craze for him at the time and used to buy English editions from a fellow who had worked abroad. Lika presented me with the ring in Izmailovo Park. She sat astride a wooden rocking horse, and I was standing looking up at her when she said:

"This is for you," and tossed me a little box.

My friends noticed us around together and soon the news reached Baliev. One day I was just finishing work in the garage, packing up to go home when a new Fiat drove up and Baliev stepped out.

"Hello, old boy! How do you like my new bus?"

"From your latest old mistress, I suppose?" I suggested crudely.

He flushed. There was a strong smell of eau de cologne around him and this irritated me even more. Just like a woman, I thought.

"No, not at all. Actually, it did belong to a friend of mine, but she gave me the car. There's just the matter of the paperwork."

Knowing Baliev, I had guessed right. Quickly he switched the conversation from this unpleasant topic.

"Listen, old man, I need your help. I know it's six already, but I'll make it up to you. I'll pay you."

"What's up?" I cut in.

"There's something rattling in the engine..."

I lifted the bonnet and soon found the trouble.

"You've decided to do without oil, then?"

"What? Really? Well, where do you put the oil?"

"You put it up your arse!"

"I always knew you were crude."

"Listen, Baliev, I'm in a hurry. Any filling station will top up your oil. Right?"

"Thanks. Incidentally, I heard about your success. Congratulations!"

"What do you mean?"

"Well, Lika, of course. You know, between you and me I was never really interested in her. Too skinny — ballerinas are all like that..."

I looked at him and thought: just one more word about her and I'll smash his fat face in. He must have sensed how I felt, yet continued:

"Listen, you don't think any intelligent woman would

get mixed up with a working class lout, do you?"

This was a dig at me, working as a mechanic. I grinned.

"Depends what sort of a woman, doesn't it, Baliev? The whores you hang around with wouldn't, of course, but then there are women who wouldn't have anything to do with a shit like you — not even once."

This was my revenge, the point being that Lika had refused to spend even one evening with him, preferring a working class type to this snob, for all his foreign finery.

He got the point.

"You really are crude, Parkin. Still, I'm not offended. Bye!"

In order to earn more money, I changed over to shift work moving freight all over the country. I needed more money now. I never bothered about money before, but now I wanted to buy Lika a fur jacket and go with her to the South for a holiday. Everything was fine. Living with her I realized that until we had met I had only played at love, I had not really loved. Until then I had never looked for anything more than pleasure in women. For the first time I wanted something more, and it was just when I realized this, when she was most precious to me, that I lost her.

That last day I was on a late shift. My mother was out of Moscow, resting in the country. Lord, how many times since then I've dreamed and relived that final day!

"What are you going to do today?" I asked her.

"Wait for you, Henry James. Oh, Baliev rang to say

there's a party on somewhere, but I don't want to go without you. Anyway, it's such a long way off, in Fili, a dreadful area. So I'll be here, at home."

I kissed the tip of her nose not knowing that I would never see her again! What followed was one long nightmare.

I got back from work as usual a little after midnight. To my amazement Lika was not home. I hung around for half an hour waiting and then recalled she had said something about a party and Baliev. I dialled his home number; to my horror he was there.

"Where's Lika?"

My tone of voice must have scared him because he began to stammer out:

"I'm sorry, I have to go in a moment. Isn't she with you? She left three hours ago. I put her in a car..."

I listened no longer, slammed the phone down, ran out and jumped into the car. Ten minutes of furious driving later I reached his place, but he'd already fled. I knew where he would be, with his 'mumsy', which was what he called his latest friend and patroness, a widow almost twice his age. It was not far to drive.

He opened the door himself; he must have known I'd track him down . I grabbed him by the lapels of his expensive suit.

"What car did you put her into in this area? Alone?" I hissed in his face. "You knew I'd be at work when you rang her. You invited her over. How could you put her in a taxi alone so late?"

"Shsh! Don't shout!" he begged. "They might hear us."

At that moment his 'mumsy' did call him.

"Which taxi did you put her in?" I gripped his suit

until it threatened to burst at the seams.

"It wasn't a taxi!" he muttered, terrified now. "It was a private car. I just hitched her a lift."

The blood rushed to my head.

"You put her in a private car in an area like that?" I shook him so violently that he trembled like a leaf. "Where's your phone?"

"Over here".

Hastily, relieved that I had let go of him, he opened a door into a luxurious sitting room where the widow, a fat woman in a Chinese dressing gown and with lots of rouge on her face, was sitting on a plush sofa in front of the television. In my dirty, oil-stained overalls, leaving a trail across the expensive pale carpet, I went over and switched off the television in front of the dumbstruck widow. Then I picked up the snow-white receiver of the telephone in one dirty hand.

"Albert, who's that?" squealed the widow, regaining the gift of speech.

"It's all right, mumsy, it's only Boris. You recognize him, don't you? There seems to have been an accident, but it wasn't my fault..."

"Keep quiet!" I roared at him.

I called the police and they came round straight away. They asked Baliev what sort of a car it was, what make, what colour, who was in it. The questioning revealed some very nasty things. He'd deceived her: she hadn't wanted to come when he rang her, so he took a taxi and picked her up, explaining that he'd rung me and that I was going to come. I'd promised.

Then at the party he got drunk and started pestering her, at which point she realized he must have deceived her and that I wasn't likely to come. She collected her bag and left, but came back a few minutes later and asked him to take her home. Their conversation, as recorded by the police, went like this:

"Albert, would you see me home? It's dreadfully dark round here and I don't think there are any taxis..."

"How about your mechanic coming and fetching you? Oh, all right, I'll get you a lift home..."

They went out and he stopped the first car that came along. As he now recalled, there were three men in it.

"Maybe you'll change your mind and stay, you must be fed up with your mechanic by now? Anyhow he won't know."

"You're a bastard!" were her last words as the car drove off.

"And you're a fool!" he yelled after her.

Now he sat in front of the police Inspector, pale, in a cold sweat of fear over his responsibility, glancing warily now and then at his widow-mumsy and explaining jerkily that he couldn't remember the number of the car, the make, the colour — nothing except that there had been three men in it. What did they look like? He couldn't remember that either.

I spent the whole night with the Inspector and his three men scouring the Fili district. We asked every pedestrian, stopped every car. Lika had vanished. A week later they fished her corpse out of the river; it was mutilated almost beyond recognition. I didn't go to identify her, I couldn't. Three days later — I still couldn't bring myself to look at the body — I buried her.

After this life lost all meaning for me. I thought at first I wouldn't survive. I don't know how I lived, I just worked on like a robot. Then my mother died. I began to drink heavily and this led me into trouble. I hit the manager of the garage where I worked. Sure, he was a lousy bastard, but I had no reason to hit him. In an effort to forget it all I changed jobs and took to long-distance driving, getting away from Moscow on long runs down south to Odessa and the other Black Sea ports. Six months later this job finished, so I came back to Moscow and found work as a driver with a construction firm. Another year and a half passed. The pain of Lika's loss was almost dulled. And yet at times memories of this past lost life suddenly loomed up — a day, a fleeting moment, a carelessly spoken word and my heart was stabbed with the bitter pain of what was gone, of the irrevocable loss. I just lived out the days at our old apartment. Admittedly, I'd changed a lot: I was reserved, shut in on myself and seldom met my old friends or invited them round. And that's how matters stood until last Thursday when I ran into him, Baliev, once again.

It was a splendid day: the sun had dried out the ground and it was very warm. We were working in a village about thirty kilometres from Moscow, building a villa settlement for the Ministry of Foreign Affairs. My job was simple: with my bulldozer I had to demolish some ramshackle old houses to clear the area for new comfortable villas meant for ministry officials. A few of these new villas had already been built off to one side, but they weren't occupied yet because there were still no roads, electricity pylons or pipes for the central heating system.

It was half past seven in the evening, but I was still working. I was putting in extra time to make up for the next day, when I had begged a couple of hours off work for an errand I had to do. Anyway, about eight I switched off the engine, got out of the cab and began to look around for somewhere to wash my hands and get a drink of water. Our office-cum-rest hut was long since closed and I was quite alone on the site. I knew there must be a stand pipe somewhere around and began to look for it. Then, about 200 metres away, somebody emerged from one of the newly-built houses and started fiddling around with the gate.

"Hey, mate!" I shouted. "Do you know where there's a tap round here? I need to wash my hands and get a drink..."

As I said this, I walked toward the man, then stopped abruptly. The blood drained from my face. The man was Baliev. I hadn't seen him since the day he'd sent Lika to her death. When he saw me he paled too but quickly recovered himself and behaved as though nothing had happend between us.

"It's you, old man! Great to see you! What are you doing around here?"

"Working," I said curtly.

I changed my mind about washing my hands; a drink of water and I'd be off.

"Can you give me some water?"

"What a question! There's wine, there's beer, there's vodka — whatever you want. Come in, this is my new abode."

"No thanks, I'll wait here. Just a glass of water."

He shrugged and went into the house, returning shortly with a mug of water. I drank and thought: how I hate this bastard. But he went on blithely boasting.

"What do you think of the house, then? Two storeys, a terrace, a garden, two-car garage, six rooms. And guess how much I paid for it?"

When he saw I couldn't care less about his property he

looked a little disappointed, but that didn't stop him from chattering on.

"My wife's back in Moscow, in our apartment," — I had heard rumours that he'd married the daughter of some senior KGB official, "and I'm here. Look, why don't you stay? You're in luck, I've got some birds coming, little ballet-girls, top notch! We've no electricity yet so we can have a ball by candle light..."

His *little ballet-girls, top notch*, made me lose all control. Suddenly I recalled how this bastard had deceived Lika, inviting her round behind my back, making a pass at her and then sticking her in a car with three murderers when she repulsed him. Completely beside myself, I ran back to my bulldozer, tore open the door and jumped into the cab. I switched on the engine and sent the great vehicle lurching towards his house.

Baliev realized at once what I was going to do. He ran back and forth in front of the vehicle like a hunted rat shouting:

"You're crazy! What are you doing? It's cost me a fortune! Stop, you fool! Help! Help!"

But there was nobody to help, there were just the two of us. Then he knelt down and begged me not to demolish his house. From the height of my driving seat he looked like a small, worthless insect that I must crush, for he had taken everything from me, he had ruined my life. I no longer heard him shouting, not just because of the noise of the engine but because I didn't want to hear him. Furiously I battered away at his villa until it collapsed like a house of cards; soon there was nothing left, only splintered wood and a heap of stones and bricks.

I sat there in the bulldozer for a while, as if turned to

95

stone. I still wonder — after all, I could have killed him, I don't know to this day how I let him live. Through some seventh sense, I'm sure, Baliev realized this.

Then I got into my car and drove back to Moscow. That same night they brought me here after Baliev rang the police. I did not blame him, he had, after all, lost his splendid new house. Why was I remembering all that now? Of course, the memory of Lika was always in my heart, she was always with me and for me alone. I'd told hardly anything of this to Max or Rolf, just the broad outlines. Nor could I share it with any of the doctors, certainly not with that bastard Loza or with Petters when they insisted I give them a clear explanation of my inexplicable behaviour. Somehow, I decided, I would outwit them; I'd get out of here without them prying into my heart and mind.

SEVENTH AND EIGHTH DAYS

11

Simon was a plumber by trade, he was also a drunkard, a brawler, and a bully. He had no morals whatsoever, no trace of principles. Like all his kind, he could be bought for a glass of vodka. He also had one peculiarity: words cascaded from his lips before a thought was born in his brain. As regards women, his views were basically sexual. It was these views, and his resultant actions, that regularly landed him up here every three or four months.

Simon was very friendly with Rakoff, the orderly, if you can call a relationship based on drinking friendship. Rakoff would bring vodka into the block, although this was strictly against regulations. Even before breakfast he would come along and collect Simon, his indispensable boozing companion, and take him off to the Recreation Room where they would have a drink.

Tippling like this from early morning only aggravated his natural aggression, so that he was always trying to pick a fight with the men. With women, his constant drinking drove him to all sorts of tricks, his favourite one being to scare the nurses.

One morning, as two young nurses were making their round of the ward to record any complaints or ailments, Simon slipped right down under the bedclothes and began to groan. When the nurses hurried over to see what was wrong, he threw off the bedclothes and displayed himself completely naked. Screaming and howling, the nurses tried to flee, but Musa, the Tartar, rushed to the door and blocked their exit. Two older nurses turned up, alerted by the row, and Musa let them in; he was very careful not to go too far in his dealings with the administration. The young nurses rushed out of the ward, still in tears. And that was it, one of Simon's pranks.

Dr Petters arrived today with two orderlies. Somehow the administration had heard that Simon had a whole tattooing kit hidden away in his mattress. At a sign from Petters one orderly made Simon sit on a chair and kept an eye on him while the other prodded around in the mattress until he had found the tattooing equipment.

"Show me where else you've tattooed yourself, Simon," Petters ordered.

"I've nothing to hide. Here..." Simon happily slipped off his trousers and presented one buttock for her inspection.

Petters leant closer — she was short-sighted — and read. "I Love You..."

The ward went very still.

"It carries on here", said Simon innocently and showed her the other buttock.

Dr Petters had no sense of humour. She leant closer still and read the rest: "... Julia, Your Sweety."

Everyone burst out laughing. Julia was Dr Petters' first name. She stiffened, and even through the thick layer of powder it was clear that she was blushing. Her lips trembled, but then — to everyone's astonishment — she simply left the room without a word. Simon got away with it; there was no punishment. Later on I thought to myself that, although outwardly she was not like a woman, something must have quivered in that dessicated body at those words. Clearly she was a very lonely person, and her continued virginity had made her excessively modest.

Rakoff continued to terrorize the old and the weak. I bet Max five roubles he wouldn't try and get his own back on me for that first night when I'd publicly thrown him out of the ward for beating Robert. A week passed. Rakoff gave me a wide berth; he was even polite. Max paid up.

Today after breakfast, while we were in the Treatment Room, Rakoff again beat up Krivin for *lounging around the ward*. He also clouted Leon with his club. If he weren't such a loony, Leon — with his strength — could have simply slaughtered the man. Rakoff's third victim today was our beloved dwarf; he had cudgelled him around the legs so hard that Robert limped for the rest of the day.

Our Loonies' Trade Union again sprang into action.

Ravich and Dutschke handed Loza a petition with forty signatures calling for Rakoff's dismissal. The result was a negative one. When he heard about the petition, Rakoff was driven to further excesses. That evening he picked on an old epileptic admitted a few days ago and hit him so savagely with his club that the old man lay groaning for a couple of hours afterwards.

"This can't go on any longer," Rolf told us.

"We should have worked him over long since," suggested Max as always.

"That's no good," I objected. "It would only make him more spiteful. Let's go and see what Ravich thinks."

We went to the Suicides Ward. Ravich, Dutschke and Kauffman were playing cards. On seeing us they stopped playing and listened to us with their full attention.

"We can only stop it by getting rid of him completely," mused our union president.

"What do you have in mind?" I asked anxiously.

"I don't mean killing him. I mean fixing up something to get the administration to dismiss him. But it won't be easy; the bosses need him and are behind his actions. So he would have to do something very wrong indeed before they dismiss him. Anyhow, that would be one way. I'll think it over for a day or two." Ravich was of course right but Max didn't understand that.

"I was against asking Ravich," grumbled Max when we got back from the Suicides Ward. "I think all his methods and theories are ridiculous. Know what he wanted to turn our Loonies' Trade Union into? A religious studies society. It's a good thing we realized what he was up to and stopped him. The Loonies Club's only job is to defend our rights, and if peaceful means won't work we've got to use our own discretion. Religion's got no place here.''

Max on the whole did not like Ravich. They were totally different characters.

Vera Cabot's interest in me continued unabated even though I had tried to put her off. She just would not leave me alone; she stopped me whenever she saw me and offered all sorts of services. Today she dragged me off again to help her — this time with the dirty linen baskets. Leon would have been the best person for this job, and would have enjoyed it, but Leon didn't interest her. She was most amiable towards me, although she was careful when Max was around. This was since I apologized for scaring her, as Loza insisted I had done. She forgave me immediately, almost before I had got the words out of my mouth. Now she chatted away to me everywhere, and everyone started to notice the attention she gave me. What they didn't know was how often she lured me into some empty office, treated me to cigarettes and coffee and even suggested I ring home. But I have nowhere and nobody to ring. So I drank her coffee and took the cigarettes for myself and my mates.

After lunch today she got me to haul some baskets of bedclothes to the linen closet. This was small and bare, just sheets and towels tipped on the floor ready to go to the laundry. I'd unloaded the last basket and was about to leave when she moved to the door and blocked my way.

"Tell me, Boris, have you a girlfriend? I'm sure you have." She looked at me quizzically with her catlike eyes, then smiled, flashing those marvellous teeth.

"I have a lot of women," I answered curtly, trying to get past, but she was so wedged in the doorway that I could not leave without brushing against her fabulous boobs. Fury rose in me. Why the hell should I resist if she wants it so much. Perhaps I should chuck her down into the corner onto those rags.

"So you like women?" she said softly. "Why do you ignore me then? Don't you like me?"

I could see she had no intention of letting me pass; she was waiting to see what I would do.

"Oh, I dream of getting inside your knickers," I took her by the waist, swung her away from the door and left. It's a good thing the linen closet was at the end of the service passage and that none of the Americans witnessed that scene.

That evening Rolf and I sat around with Ravich talking about life. He is very sparing with his words, and I liked that. He did not like to talk about himself not because he was secretive, but because of his great modesty; he did not consider himself sufficiently important. Besides he had had an experience which nearly cost him his life and taught him that indeed silence can be golden.

"Why are you always so silent?" I asked him. "You never join in the conversation."

"If it's a conversation that's leading nowhere, even

one word is superfluous," he replied, fixing me with his thoughtful light eyes.

"You told us once you wanted to settle right out in the country, far away from people. What's wrong with Moscow? After all, you were born here..." Rolf asked him.

"The city, my friends is a complex of selfish attitudes. I don't like people: they're too envious, too militant and too concerned with their own interests. Long ago I decided that modern civilization must have developed from selfish attitudes and is maintained only by constant terror and force. Nowadays everything serves the purpose of war, that mindless beast. There's no discovery the military won't put to some use. There's no war going on at present, but we have a peace armed to the teeth. Man has wreaked every evil he can contrive against nature — look at the devastation and pollution he's caused — and against his fellow man. The outcome is the triumph of evil and the dominion of death on earth. It all goes to show the logical defect in all those utopias that are so concerned with future generations, with those who don't yet exist. What about those they've killed off, why forget about them? And what sort of a kingdom of bliss would it be if this senseless force of death still remained?"

Suddenly the ironic gleam faded from his eyes; for a while he sucked silently on his pipe, then abruptly excused himself and left.

"Well," said Rolf, "it's very interesting to listen to him."

Talking with Ravich refreshed my spirit and mind and it was not till later, when I thought more about it, that the tragic meaning of his words really struck me. After all, what he had been saying about the city and the selfish attitude of people in cities was what I had thought myself, when I decided to abandon everything to get away from the rat race.

We were all well settled in bed when we heard frantic screams from the corridor.

"They're beating somebody up," Robert jumped over the foot of the bed and dashed out of the ward. A few moments later he was back in the doorway, white as a sheet, yelling:

"It's Rakoff, fellows! He's killing Krivin..."

We all dashed out into the corridor, but it was too late. We heard the door to the service passage click to. Krivin was lying on the floor of the Treatment Room, his head split open and one eye rolled right up; the other had burst out of its socket. Later we heard that all the vertebrae in his neck had been broken. They took him straight off to surgery but soon brought him back. He lay in his bed, his head and neck all bandaged, his hands like two pale twin creatures on the blanket.

"Should call a priest, but being the heathen he is, Marx is all he cares about," mumbled old Dementich, "... and anyway, this scum here, torturing Christian people, they wouldn't allow it neither." This was the doctors he referred to.

Towards morning, without regaining consciousness, Grisha Krivin died. That night nobody in the ward slept. We stood around Krivin's bed as though waiting for something. Even the Count and his cronies abandoned their cards and huddled together whispering. Evidently they were just realizing that the atmosphere in the ward had reached flashpoint and that we outnumbered them.

Robert spent the whole time sitting by Grigory's feet, his little arms folded across his chest. Nobody could get him to leave. He was taking it as keenly as though they had killed not some stranger but the girl he loved. Yes, God may have created him a freak and ruined his life, but he had not grown bitter. Quite the reverse; his personal misfortune had made him a true altruist, kindness itself.

In the morning, long before breakfast, we heard the strains of music. It was Sasha Feldman playing some very sad air on the piano in the Recreation Room. Old Dementich had taken it upon himself to open it ahead of time. The sound soon attracted the doctors, but nobody said anything to the old man. Dr Petters was more curt than usual; she did not know what to expect, how the administration would react. From us she expected nothing but trouble. Soon Krivin was taken away, and we saw him no more.

After breakfast Ravich, Dutschke and Alyosha, our best negotiators went off to see Loza. They soon returned, disappointed.

"Rakoff has written a statement that Krivin attacked him first. He says he's got bites on his hand to prove it," said Alyosha.

"Loza also showed us some paper claiming that Krivin died from a burst blood vessel. Says he had a bad heart," added Dutschke.

"It's all Ravich's fault," said Max to us bitterly after the engineer had left. "He's always trying to use persuasion and peaceful means, but as you can see, with criminals they don't work. If we had dealt with Rakoff ourselves, none of this would have happened."

I did not sympathize with Max's methods, but I had no answer to this. Everyone else went off for their walk but I was summoned to Loza's office. What do they want now? I opened the door. Sitting at the department head's desk was Vera Cabot, smiling.

12

"Boris, I need to listen to your chest and take one or two samples. Get undressed and sit on the couch behind the screen." She acted as though there had been nothing between us and she had not been familiar with me, nor I with her. I wondered why she had got me along to Loza's office instead of the Treatment Room where all the tests are usually carried out. She was up to something again.

"Take off everything except your underpants," she said as I went behind the screen.

I was undressed and sitting on the couch when she appeared.

"I'll take your blood pressure first. Give me your arm."

She sat down next to me, bound a sort of black strip round my upper arm, pumped it up and looked at the gauge.

"Your blood pressure's very good. Give me your other arm."

She took blood from one finger and another blood sample from a vein. Then she began to tap me on the chest, looking up now and again into my face. She was wearing some good perfume, and the scent set my head spinning.

"After the May Day holiday I'll have to start giving you aminazine tablets," she said very seriously. "Do you have any idea what they are?"

"No".

"Well, if you take them regularly they can have an inhibitive effect. You understand? I mean, when you're with a woman... I don't want to give you them and that's why I've got you along here to have a talk. Petters is in the Treatment Room all day today." She stopped and looked at me.

"I understand, but what makes you so concerned about me? And how am I meant to pay you back?"

Suddenly she threw her arms round my neck, hugged me and whispered:

"I'm in love with you. Can't you see that? I took a fancy to you right from the start... I'm going mad about you."

From this close range I stared at her face: a beautiful, wanton face, large sensual mouth, straight short nose, fine nervous nostrils quivering like a young throughbred horse. Nostrils that were too nervous for her.

"What do you want from me? Need me for your collection?" I said crudely, remembering all Rolf had told me about her.

107

"Oh, forget it!" She stood up suddenly, smoothed her hair and left the office.

To kill time I began to jot down everything that had happened to me, right from the very first day. Max managed to get me an exercise book and a fountain pen. At first I wrote it straight down, just trying to keep to the facts, but later I got carried away with the job. I began to re-read what I had written, crossing out bits and putting in more details. Once Rolf caught me at this.

"What are you writing? A novel?"

"Well, sort of. I'm trying to write down what's happened to me..."

"Good idea. Let's have a look."

I handed him the exercise book. He opened the first page and read: THE AMERICANS.

"Aha, about us, is it?"

I smiled.

"Then you'd better call it..." He thought for a moment. "We were Three Men..."

"And One Tall Dwarf." I ended it for him.

We both burst out laughing. At that moment Robert appeared in the doorway and asked us to come along and talk to Max in the toilets. I shut the book and hid it under my mattress.

In the toilets Max Whitley was sitting on a window ledge, smoking and evidently furious. The three of us came in and waited for him to start. Max stubbed his cigarette out against the wall and asked gloomily:

"What are we going to do about that bastard, Rakoff?"

"Give him a good hiding!" urged Rolf.

"Sure," I agreed.

"Well, I think we should settle him for good," said Max.

"What do you mean?" I asked.

"Nothing — yet, but I want all of you to think it over and give me your suggestions this evening. Oh, yes, I nearly forgot; to give you an idea how urgent it is I ought to mention that he's just had a real go at Robert."

Rolf and I stared at one another in amazement. Why hadn't the dwarf mentioned it? We looked at him, but Robert said nothing. It was only now that we noticed he had a black eye and a big bruise near his left ear. Hunched up, he seemed even smaller. His flabby little cheeks trembled and he could barely hold back his tears.

"Whitley, I'll give you my answer right now," I said firmly. "I'm against any lynching. You want to drag yourself down to his level? But rough him up a bit — yes!"

Rolf said nothing and I sensed he didn't support me. Rolf's a fine fellow but he's got one serious defect. He's too easily influenced. Now he is completely under Max's thumb, and Max is a real tough character. He's capable of really crazy things; he flares up easily and then it's hard to stop him. There's no question about Robert — he has always been led by Max. As for me — sometimes

Max and I are close, and at other times I have to put some distance between us. Max was disappointed that he couldn't control or influence me. He's a man who likes to dominate others, and I sometimes think that hardheartedness is his main characteristic. He's also jealous of me because of Vera Cabot, although he knows I'm not really interested in her. Shouldn't get jealous, but it's there all the same. If he had any real grounds, I don't know what he'd do. As I said, he's capable of really crazy things.

Saturday dragged on in boredom. First of all, it was a gloomy day and secondly, I was filled with gloomy thoughts. When I get out of here, I'll get myself some well paid job up north and settle up with Baliev.

During our exercise period I trained a bit with Max and Rolf for tomorrow's match and forgot my misery for a while. Then we went to the bath-house and the barbers. Because of the May Day holiday, they'd switched our time from Sunday to Saturday. On the way back I saw Dementich in the corridor. He was sitting on a bench reading a paper, his metal-rimmed glasses bound with string perched on the end of his nose. I sat down next to him and glanced at the paper.

"What's this, Dementich? You believe in God yet you read a party newspaper."

"Believe nothing! They've done away with God, so now I'm like everyone else," he muttered.

"How come, Dementich? You used to believe..."

"Used to, but I don't no more. God's sinful if he lets them get away with this filthy Hell."

"What do you mean?"

"What d'ye mean? What d'ye mean? Yesterday they knocked off the Marxist, and tomorrow they'll do somebody else in. What's he doing up there, just watching? And that Vietnam war going on and on..." He stabbed the paper with his finger. "I fought the Krauts, I know what war's like — the devil's work, it is. Look at the times we live in: people are worse than beasts. No, that's not being fair to beasts: no beast touches its own kind, but man... He'll wipe his own kind out with guns, bombs, anything he can lay his hands on..."

I'd no answer to that. The old man was right, wasn't he? Krivin was tortured here, then killed. But Rakoff will probably get some May Day commendation for his *good work*. Criminal proceedings? Forget it!

"I'll tell you how it is with God and me. It's a secret, mind," the old man leant closer. "I don't know what to do with him now. Seems like I always believed in him — at home, of course, not at work. I've been looking for truth, but now, after the Marxist, I've begun to have my doubts. I say to myself: just do what they tell you..."

That night again I couldn't sleep. My head reeled with dreadful images: first I was chasing somebody, now they were tracking me down with dogs, then I fell into some snow. Snow? Where the hell had that come from if this was May Day?

111

NINTH DAY

In the morning one could see the clouds through the window growing whiter, stretching out, curling into braids and beyond the blue which appeared on the horizon, one could see the first of the sun's rays. It was evidently going to be very warm. Before lunch we bustled about preparing for the celebrations. The Americans were very happy to greet the spring, but what had spring to do with them, locked in this cage? Right after breakfast they got us to clear up and decorate the large Recreation Hall on the ground floor, hanging flags and slogans that Alyosha had painted with white paint on red cloth. The slogans had been composed by Ustinov, the man who had voluntarily returned from America. They were mere doggerel, although Ustinov fancied himself as a poet and spent all his spare time writing. After one session of his poems I came to the conclusion he really must be a bit crazy. He'd pestered everyone with his poems, the trouble being that all his poems had one theme only — America and how nice it was to live there. You just couldn't stop him. Most of all he pestered Robert, who was too well-mannered to say a harsh word to anyone. Holding him on his lap, he would churn out his verses for hours at a time. Now, whenever he saw Ustinov coming, Robert would hide behind us. The second time he tried to read me his poems, I told him: "Listen, mate. Piss off!" Since then he'd been feeling deeply offended by me, and left me alone. Still his poems swamped the ward newspaper that Dr Petters ran. It was she who got him to make up some ubsolutely crazy medical slogans.

During lunch Rakoff unexpectedly appeared in the canteen: since Krivin's death he had kept well out of our way. Whitley snarled, and Rolf hissed: "He's coming this way!"

He was all got up in his Sunday best. Beneath his hospital smock he was wearing a new suit and a white shirt with a white tie. His hair was neatly brushed. Rakoff was not carrying his club: I don't think he would have dared appear before us with that so soon after all that had happened. He halted by the next table, deterred from coming any closer by the fierce look on Max's face.

"Hello, lads! May Day greetings to you!" he said to us.

We stared back silently — all, that is, except for the well-bred Robert who answered: "And the same to you."

Rakoff took this as a sign of forgiveness on our part and beamed all over his face. Whitley refused to look at him; he turned his back and scrutinized a crack in the ceiling. Rakoff stood there, shifting from foot to foot, utterly at a loss how to get into conversation with us.

Then he left. Max snarled an obscenity after him.

After lunch we hung around the Recreation Room waiting for permission to go out. Today was the day of the football match. Rakoff reappeared, but this time Robert drew him aside.

"What do you want, midge?" asked Rakoff quite genially.

We stood and listened.

"Have you got a corkscrew, Rakoff?" asked the dwarf quite straightfaced.

Rakoff pricked up his ears.

"What for then?"

"Well, Max's mother brought us something for May Day, but we don't have a corkscrew."

"What you got, vodka?" the orderly licked his lips.

"No... Something better."

Rakoff's cheeks flushed.

"Whisky," said the dwarf softly but quite distinctly.

"Get away! Let's have a look!"

"Please show him, Max," said the dwarf.

We huddled around to shield Max from the others in the room. From the inside pocket of his jacket he extracted a bottle with a foreign label. A yellowy liquid glinted in the sunlight.

"Fuck me, that's really something!" Rakoff was astounded.

"So you can give us a corkscrew?" the dwarf asked. "You're invited, of course."

"Sure, lads, sure. When?"

"Today, while the film's on, when everybody's in the big hall."

"Right. You're on."

13

At exactly four o'clock our two teams — the Suicides
and the Americans — filed out into the yard, where a
hundred or so fans were already waiting. The only ones
missing were the bed patients and the real loonies, and
they wouldn't really have appreciated the event properly.
The whole staff of the hospital had also turned out to
watch — doctors, nurses, orderlies and even the cleaners
— after all, nobody wanted to miss a football match
between *madmen*. Even so these were only a small
proportion of the spectators: most of them were watching from behind the barred windows of the Violent
Wing. The women, too, had been kept away in view
of the recent fraternization incident. Still they clustered
at the windows of their block, blowing us kisses.

The twenty-two players took the field: the Americans in white vests with red stripes on the back and
white stars in one corner, the emblem of the American
flag. The Suicides were in black vests decorated with a
skull and crossbones — the idea of Alyosha, who had
designed both costumes.

Our captains — Pete Dutschke for the Suicides and Max
for the Americans — shook hands, and the goalkeepers
ran to their places. The Americans' goalkeeper was
Robert, a most controversial choice against which many
had objected because of his tiny stature and short arms,
but Max had insisted. He believed in Robert because

he was a good circus acrobat. So now our dwarf stood in the goal looking very serious. He was dressed in a striped black and white sweater and fiery red boots, the ones he wore at the circus. His dwarf girlfriend has brought them over specially for the match.

The referee had been recruited specially from a neutral block, the Drug Addicts'. He whistled the game off and immediately the Suicides launched a furious attack on our goal. Nearly all the first half was fought in our penalty area. The Suicides pressed hard and our defence was fully stretched trying to beat off the attack. Ten minutes before half time Mike Kauffman, one of the Suicides' forwards, dodged our full backs, Vic Kotik and Marc Lerner, passed to one-eyed Ivan, a soldier who had shot his own eye out — and he kicked the ball at the top corner. Robert jumped with all his might, but the ball streaked past his short arms and thudded into our net.

At half time Max paced around, black as a thunder cloud. We learned from our fans that Kauffman had sworn to put in at least a dozen goals. Rolf advised Max to replace Robert, but Max shook his head and smoked silently on. With a goalkeeper like this we were in a bad way, and to make matters worse one of our defenders, Ustinov, slipped at the last minute and twisted his ankle. We had to replace him with our reserve, Alyosha, who had had little experience and trained only at the last minute. Because of this Max had moved Rolf back to the defence to cover Alyosha and put Vic Kotik in his place among forwards.

Right at the start of the second half Max neatly took the ball off the Suicides's forward Nikita, a shortish one-armed soldier, dodged several defenders and passed the ball to me. I passed to Rolf, Rolf back to Max and Max safely netted the ball in our opponents' goal.

Our fans howled with glee. We had evened the score, and our spirits rose. After this the Suicides tried to regain the initiative. In the fourteenth minute Kauffman again weaved through our defence and belted the ball at our goal. But this time Robert leapt like a springheeled jack and picked the ball out of the air.

Our fans again howled with delight. Later we were told that the doctors were clutching their stomachs with helpless laughter and Loza had tears rolling down his fat cheeks from so much mirth. From a window of the women's wing somebody tossed Robert a tiny bunch of violets.

The second half of the game was bitterly fought. We simply couldn't break through the Suicides' defence until, fifteen minutes before the end, Kauffman committed two bad fouls, kicking Vic Kotik on the leg and tripping Rolf. Vic fell to the ground and it was some minutes before he could get to his feet. Play stopped while a doctor examined him, but it was not too serious. Limping badly, Vic got to his feet and carried on. The public howled its disgust and the referee ordered an eleven metres penalty kick.

We lined up in front of their goal. There was a deathly silence as Max raced up to the ball and blasted it into the net. The score was now 2—1 to us. We danced around the field hugging each other but the referee whistled the game on. In the last few minutes the Suicides regained the initiative and Dutschke dribbled the ball around Rolf and Marc Lerner and kicked for goal, but once again Robert leapt and took the ball.

The roar from the crowd was indescribable. In their excitement the loonies at the windows of the Violent Wing tugged at each other's hair. The Suicides made one last furious attack to at least even the score, but our forwards again intercepted the ball. Passing and feinting, Max and I dodged all Dutschke's players until, right in front of the enemy's goal, I found myself in an excellent position. Rolf passed me the ball and yelled: "Shoot!" I put everything I had into the shot, and the ball rocketed into the net. Next moment the referee blew the final whistle. The match between the Americans and the Suicides had ended in a complete victory for us.

We hugged and kissed each other, our fans rushed out onto the field and began to embrace us too. Suddenly there was a shout: "Stop him!" A naked man raced out of one of the doors and began to tear about the field, three orderlies chasing after him with blankets. It was one of the patients from the Violent Wing. He had tired of watching the match from a window, evaded the orderly in charge and managed to sneak out. He was soon caught, trussed, covered with blankets, and carted back into the block. The incident was soon forgotten.

We continued to celebrate our victory. The main hero, of course, was Robert, whom Max carried into the canteen to general cheers. Within fifteen minutes the nurses brought us a stack of letters from our women admirers, including three drug addicts who offered to marry Robert. Robert was the happiest person in the world and perhaps for the first time in his life felt he was a real man: here were three normal-sized women offering to marry him.

For supper the players from both teams were given an extra portion of potatoes sprinkled with something very like mince. Today was the first time that I had finished supper without still feeling hungry. Many of our fans brought us presents — an apple, a piece of bread with real butter, some sugar. I ended up with three apples, two pieces of bread and butter and four lumps of sugar.

Straight after supper we were herded along to the Recreation Hall for a May Day party. As we came in, the table on the stage underneath the portraits of Brezhnev, Kosygin and others was already occupied by Loza, Dr Petters, Vera Cabot and two more doctors whom I didn't know. Fortunately, the speeches were short — evidently the administration had decided that propaganda was a pointless exercise for lunatics, for after the brief official speeches we were entertained with a concert.

The first number was a dance by two Suicides — Nikita, the one-armed soldier, and one-eyed Ivan — while Dutschke accompanied them on the accordion. Everybody greatly enjoyed the dance. Then came a song from another soldier, lacking a foot which he had hacked off himself. He had a fine, strong voice. After that it was Robert's turn. He appeared on the stage in a broad-brimmed hat and a long black robe decorated with small stars. He was like some fantastic dwarf from an Anderson fairy tale. Robert ran through a number of tricks such as asking somebody to blindfold him, then showing the audience a number of cards which he correctly named. After that he asked Dr Loza to come up onto the stage, offered him a chair, chatted with him for a few minutes and then asked him what he had in the inside pockets of his jacket.

"Oh, identity card, money, party membership card, and a ticket to the theatre..." said the head of the department.

Robert asked him to take everything out and show them to the audience. Loza did as he was asked but couldn't find his party membership card. This made him very upset. Then Robert produced the card from his sleeve. Loza was amazed, overjoyed and emded up weeping with laughter.

But the greatest success of the evening was Sasha Feldman, who appeared on stage with his violin which Loza had allowed to be brought from his home for the occasion. Sasha put the violin to his chin; drew the bow across it and out came a spellbinding melody. The entire hall was hushed, even the breathing. I'm not an expert in music, but he played something extremely sad, something unworldly, and I realized that Sasha must be a brilliant musician.

The applause was long, and there were many calls for an encore, but Sasha stepped down from the stage and I saw him hand his violin to old Dementich. The concert ended with a choral rendering of "Moscow Nights", sung by twenty men under the direction of Ustinov. Leon also sang in the choir. There was a four-piece jazz-band: Sasha Feldman on the piano, Dutschke on the accordion, Vic Kotik on the electric guitar, and Robert on drums.

After the concert the same band played for the dance. Apart from Dr Petters and two middle-aged nurses there were no women present: Vera Cabot had gone off somewhere, much to the distress of Max who had counted on dancing with her. So we all danced with each other, and the Suicide jazz fanatic danced with himself. After that the doctors and nurses went off for their party in Loza's office, leaving us under the supervision of old Dementich and two middle-aged female orderlies.

After a while a scuffle broke out when the Count began pestering Alyosha, who had sat quietly in a corner sketching the dancers. Alyosha politely declined the Count's call to come and dance, whereupon the Count tore the sketch-book from his grasp and began to drag him onto the floor by force. The fragile Alyosha resisted as best he could, but the Count propelled him along with hearty kicks in the backside. Suddenly the band fell silent and Sasha descended from the stage. His eyes flashing with anger.

"Leave him alone, Count, or we won't play..."

At once the Count let Alyosha go, grabbed Sasha by the lapels and hissed: "What fucking business is it of yours, Jewboy?"

Sasha went pale, then tore himself loose and slapped the Count across the face with all his strength. It was so sudden that the Count gaped and stood there for a moment, dumbfounded, then hit Sasha full in the face with his fist, flattening him against the wall. Sasha slid to the floor and was trying to regain his feet when the Count swung back to kick him in the face. At that moment Rolf intervened; he grabbed the leg and sent the Count sprawling on the floor.

Seeing that they were attacking one of his kind, even though a rival, Gipsy whistled up his gang and we found ourselves involved in a free-for-all with the criminals. Chairs flew through the air. Musa flattened Vic Kotik with a chair leg and Ustinov got a terrible jab in the eye. Robert pounded his drums and yelled: "Get them! Give it to them!"

There were more of us, and we soon had them pinned against the wall and would have really finished them if it hadn't been for the doctors, summoned by the terrified female orderlies. On Loza's orders, the male orderlies piled into us and soon gained the upper hand. After that Loza lined us up and began to investigate who had started the affair. We said nothing, but Simon burst out and claimed that Sasha Feldman had begun the fight. Kotik, Kauffman and Mayer yelled that this was all bloody lies, that Sasha was innocent and had only been standing up for Alyosha, whom the Count had been pestering. Loza wouldn't listen to them. Two orderlies grabbed Sasha and dragged him out of the hall. Then Loza announced:

"This time I'll forgive you. I don't want to deprive you of a treat just because of one hooligan. As planned, we will now have a newsreel, followed by a feature film."

Everybody cheered, forgetting immediately about Sasha. Benches were carried into the hall, everybody found a seat, the screen was lowered and the lights dimmed. Max nudged me: "Let's go!"

Unnoticed we slipped out of the hall.

14

When we got to the ward, Robert and Rolf were already there, but there was no sign of Rakoff.

"Doesn't look like he's coming," said Rolf anxiously.

"He'll come," muttered Max.

I knew they meant to squeeze a good price out of him for a bottle of fake whisky. They made it by diluting vodka with lemon juice and flavouring it with mustard and pepper. This revolting mixture they had decanted into a foreign bottle, not whisky, but wine, which did not matter since the orderly knew no English. I was also sure they wouldn't confine themselves to just selling him this stuff; they would probably beat him up. I thought with a bastard like him that would be only right and proper if it succeeded in destroying his delight in beating up others. Thoughts like these were running through my head when I heard footsteps and went to meet him by the door leading to the service passage.

"Hi, you're here, then." Rakoff was pink with excitement. "I couldn't get away earlier. That old bitch Petters would have me sit next to her for the film and I had a hell of a job getting away. Anyway, let's start. Here's the corkscrew."

From his pocket he extracted a penknife and opened the corkscrew gadget. Max put the bottle on a chair and began to open it, while Robert held a paper cup all ready. At last Max had the bottle open.

"Okay, pour it out," said the orderly.

"Let's see the money first."

"Sure, lads, just as I promised."

He was so excited he had a hard time finding the money in his pockets, but at last he fished out a wad of crumpled banknotes and counted several off.

"Here you are, twenty-five roubles. Better check it."

Max leafed through the notes and stuck them in his pocket.

"All the whisky's yours. We decided it was only right to sell you the whole bottle. But only on condition you drink it here; it would be dangerous to take it out."

"Oh, sure. Thanks, lads. Anything you like."

Robert poured him the first shot and Rakoff took the cup with trembling hands.

"Better lock the doors, just in case. We don't want anybody coming in," urged Max.

"Good thinking," the orderly stopped with the cup halfway to his lips. He had not noticed Whitley's tone of voice. "They'd chuck me out if they found I'd been drinking with the patients."

Carefully, anxious not to spill a drop, he put the cup down on a chair and went to close the door. He also locked the other door which led to the Recreation Room and then on to the Suicides Ward.

"Right, now we're okay."

"What about there?" asked Max, turning to the dwarf and pointing to the door to the Treatment Room.

"There's nobody there," said Robert.

"Have you looked?"

"Yes. It's dark and there's nobody there."

"So let's get on with it," said Rakoff impatiently, raising the cup to his lips and inhaling deeply.

"Phew! Strong stuff!" He tipped back the cup.

We all froze.

"I've never tasted anything like that before," said the orderly slowly, then smiled and let out an oath which in his book was the height of approval.

"So it's good stuff, is it?" asked Robert.

"First-rate! God, I've never drunk anything like it."

"It's Irish whisky. Max's mother's just back from Ireland," said Robert and poured a second cupful, which the orderly downed at one go and wiped his lips on his sleeve. In this manner he soon polished off the entire bottle.

"Right, Rakoff! Now get in that corner," said Whitley grimly.

"Eh, what for?" asked the orderly bemusedly.

"Get in the corner, you bastard."

Grabbing the orderly by the lapels of his overall, he threw him against the wall.

"What are you up to, lads? What's the matter?"

"You're under arrest, that's what's the matter," said Rolf.

He took a piece of paper from his pocket and read: "For persistent abuse of the weak, the old and the sick, also for the murder of Grigory Krivin, former university lecturer, the senior orderly of the Seventh Department, Mikhail Rakoff, is hereby sentenced to death by hanging. This sentence is not subject to appeal and will be executed immediately."

Rakoff went as pale as chalk. In a few moments he had changed utterly, his arms and legs trembled. Suddenly he fell to his knees.

"Don't, lads! I didn't mean to. It was him — he bit me, fucking commie, on the hand and I gave him a little tap, just enough to scare him. He died because he was sick, see. He had this bad heart. That's what Loza said; it's all down on the papers. It wasn't my fault, I swear."

"Get up, you shit!" Whitley grabbed him by the

125

shoulders and hauled him to his feet, but Rakoff fell back to his knees. "Take him out!" Max ordered Rolf.

Rolf dragged Rakoff into the toilets. The orderly resisted as best he could and Rolf had to drag him along the floor. Max brought in the chair on which he had just opened Rakoff's bottle of *whisky*. They tied his hands and legs with a piece of electric flex.

Rakoff resisted, then began to weep. Rolf punched him on the jaw and he shut up.

I realized I must act. These idiots really meant to kill him.

"That's enough, Whitley. You've scared him, now let him go."

He turned to me.

"I know you'd come over all tearful. You're a decent bloke, Parkin, but sometimes you can be a real prick. Evil's got to be rooted out. Yesterday he killed Krivin, tomorrow he could go at you with a knife. Don't you understand that?"

"What's this? Are you really serious? You're out of your minds. I thought you meant to scare him — well, rough him up a bit. But murder? Ravich would never go for that. Stop it!"

He went up to Rolf and whispered something in his ear. Rolf turned to me.

"Sorry, friend, we all like you but we won't let you stop us carrying out a just sentence. We're going to have to tie you up — for a while, of course. I hope you won't struggle or kick up a fuss. You don't want to get us all arrested."

They tied my arms and legs with more of the electric flex they had used on Rakoff and put me by the wall in the corridor, right opposite the *place of execution*. It was then I realized that Whitley was really crazy. They were actually going to kill him. In terms of justice I hated this bastard, but I was opposed to killing. After all, they could have given him a beating he would have remembered for the rest of his life, but killing... But they had reckoned right. I couldn't bring myself to fight them: the noise might have attracted people and we would all have been arrested and then they would have been sent off to labour camps. Idiots! Idiots! But perhaps I could still talk them out of it...

"Are you all out of your minds? Stop it! Think of the consequences," I appealed to them desperately.

"Forgive me," sobbed Rakoff.

"Stick him on the chair and get his belt," ordered Whitley.

"What are you doing? Stop it! I need my belt, else my trousers'll fall down." The orderly still didn't believe the worst was to happen.

Rolf silently unbuckled his belt and slipped it out of the loops. Slowly his trousers slid down to his ankles. Rakoff protested frantically.

"Give me my belt back! What are you doing?"

"You won't need it any more. Anyway there are no ladies present," cut in Whitley grimly.

"Spare me, lads. Mercy!"

Suddenly the door to the Treatment Room swung open. The execution was halted and we all froze. At once Rakoff seized on the distraction to topple off the chair onto the floor. Through the door of the Treatment Room appeared Simon, the plumber. He stretched sleepily, his hair dishevelled. He seemingly got drunk early on and had gone to the Treatment Room to sleep it off on the couch.

Max turned angrily on the dwarf.

"It was dark in there," lisped Robert, shrinking under his gaze. "I thought there was nobody there..."

"I told you to check, not think," hissed Max furiously.

"I'm sorry, it was my fault. I was sure there was nobody there."

"What are you fellows up to?" mumbled the plumber, scratching his head, as yet quite unaware of what was going on.

At last, as he got nearer, he noticed his mate bound hand and foot and with his trousers round his ankles, and me trussed up on the floor. Instantly sober, he dashed for the door.

"They're all locked, Simon." Whitley had such menace in his voice that the plumber went pale and pressed against the wall. "Well, since you're here, you'd better stay and watch. But quietly. Let's get on with it."

Rolf hauled Rakoff back onto the chair. This time the orderly realized that nothing was going to save him; he submitted in silence. Whitley jumped up and hooked the buckle of Rakoff's belt round a bent nail. I hadn't noticed it before; they had prepared everything well.

"Stop, you crazy fools!" I shouted. "Stop it, let him go! You've scared him for the rest of his life. He'll never touch anybody again. You won't achieve anything this way. There's enough bloodshed in the world without this."

But they wouldn't listen to me. For a moment I thought they might gag me with a towel; Whitley was quite capable of it. Suddenly Rakoff began to howl. Rolf looked anxiously at Whitley.

"Let's get it over with."

Rolf looped the belt round Rakoff's neck.

"Spare me, mates! Help! They're ki..."

Whitley had kicked the chair from under him, choking off his words. The orderly jerked and swung. For a few seconds more his thin body twitched and shuddered. Then it was all over.

Rolf untied the orderly's arms and legs; now it looked just like suicide. They smashed the foreign wine bottle, carefully picked up the bits of glass and wrapped them in some paper which Max then put in his pocket. Next to the *suicide* they tossed an ordinary vodka bottle. Then, avoiding my eye, Rolf untied me. I was silent; after all what could I say? I felt our paths had parted. Once again I had nobody, no friends, no-one. I looked at them pityingly and wondered what they intended to do to keep Simon quiet. Just threaten him, or do away with him too? This was a definite possibility, for Simon was expendable and a very dangerous witness. But Max confined himself to threats.

"Listen, filth, you squeal one word about this and I'll kill you... Get me? If I have to come back from the grave, I'll do you!" He made a gesture of slitting his throat.

"Okay, okay, Whitley, I get you." The plumber's lips trembled — he too had obviously thought they might do him in.

"Let's get the hell out of here," urged Max. "One at a time."

With Rakoff's keys he unlocked the door, let us out, tossed the keys into the toilets and slammed the door shut. One by one we got to the ground floor, and slipped into the big hall through different doors. Nobody noticed us.

The film was still under way when somebody came bursting into the hall and yelled:

"Rakoff's hung himself in the Americans' toilets!"

The lights went up immediately and the film stopped. Everybody rushed to our ward. Calmly, without batting an eyelid, Max, Rolf and the dwarf went along with the crowd.

15

The next quarter of an hour brought terrific commotion as Loza, Petters, Vera Cabot and several doctors from other departments arrived on the scene. They stood silently and looked, then left. Rakoff was taken down and carried away. After that the Suicides were ordered straight to their ward and the doors between us locked. Petters came back with two orderlies and spent a long time searching the toilets. The orderlies extracted the bent nail and took it away as evidence. Shortly after they had left, Petters returned and although it was not yet eleven, shooed us to our beds.

I lay in my bed with a book, carefully avoiding Whitley's eyes. Nobody had any thought of sleep, everybody was talking about Rakoff. They were all glad to be rid of him and it was clear from the conversation that nobody doubted he had hanged himself. Old Dementich, our friend, came into the ward and everybody rushed to ask what the administration thought about the business.

"What's think? They think he went on the booze and hung himself. All but Petters — she's dead suspicious, says she was sitting with him in the film half an hour before and he was sober then. So when did he get drunk enough to hang himself, she asks. Thinks there's something fishy about it. But what's the use puzzling over a rat like him? Of course the bastard hanged himself."

I listened and thought, if Simon didn't give us away, the doctors might never suspect he had been hanged. Especially when they opened him up tonight and found him boozed up to the gills. I noticed I was thinking now about *us* and not *them*, linking myself with *them* in this moment of danger. I was still against the lynching; I was sure Rakoff hadn't been beyond saving. He was young and corrupted by being given a free hand to abuse his power. In normal circumstances a type like him could have done no harm; he would have worked in a factory somewhere and spent his evenings in front of the television or in some bar. He was like thousands of others. But now, I couldn't just dissociate myself from my friends. I figured that since I had not found the means to stop them, I must bear the responsibility with them, although I was not going to let them know that just yet.

TENTH AND ELEVENTH DAYS

That night I fell asleep at once and slept right through until half past seven, probably because the Count didn't launch into his usual singing routine at six o'clock. Upset at the death of his friend, perhaps? Apparently not.

"The Count's stopped playing the loony. No point ruining your throat when they're sending you back to camp in a week's time anyway. Seems they told him yesterday," said Max, seeing I was awake. He spoke as though nothing had passed between us.

I made no reply; I had no wish to talk to him. The day passed calmly. It seemed as though the doctors suspected nothing and had accepted Rakoff's death as suicide.

Out on our walk my comrades suddenly came up to me, evidently wanting to make up after yesterday.

"Think he'll split on us?" Rolf nodded towards Simon. He said *us*, obviously counting me in.

"I don't know. Quite possibly."

"Well, if he does, we're finished."

"If we're for the chop, I'll do the bastard first," snarled Max.

I was quite certain he was capable of killing again.

"There's been enough killing," said Rolf firmly.

"I still don't understand how Simon got to be in the Treatment Room."

Max looked angrily at Robert.

"It was my fault. I thought there was nobody there. You can do what you want with me," whispered the dwarf in a desperate sort of voice.

"No point going over all that again," Rolf tried to reassure Robert. "Now we can only wait. And we'd best not get into huddles like this. Might cause suspicion."

We split up and went our different ways. Rolf dribbled a ball around the yard; he always got over his troubles quickly. The whole day Max never took his eyes off Simon, giving him such looks I was surprised that Simon, with his cowardly nature, didn't faint from fear.

That evening they took Leon away and transferred him to the more relaxed Thirty Second Department where I was supposed to have gone. Leon didn't want to go and even began to cry.

"Let's go, son," Dementich urged him.

"I'm frightened."

"Frightened of what?"

"I don't know."

"It's great there, Leon. Nice fresh air. You can walk in the park all day and you can make flowers in the workshop. Wouldn't you like to make some little flowers?"

"Little flowers?" Leon smiled. "Yes, I would. Can we take Ninochka?"

"Of course."

"Let's go then."

It was later I realized I had lost Lika's ring. It had always been a bit loose on my finger, but I had never lost it before. I looked for it everywhere, shaking out all the bedding and hunting on the floor. The ring was nowhere to be found and I was very upset. After supper, as we were all lounging around in the corridor, Dementich came up to me.

"They're giving the fiddler insulin. He resisted, see, so they gave him insulin."

I froze.

"Want to come and see him?"

"Of course."

"Right, then, but quietly."

Very cautiously we made our way along the service passage out of our department. We turned and twisted along various corridors until we stopped before a very solid-looking door.

"We've got to go through the Violent Wing..."

The old man opened the door and I felt a shift in reality. We had entered a world of phantoms. Already in the doorway my nostrils were assaulted by a stench which almost knocked me out. It was a smell of urine, excrement and rotten food. Pulling myself together and hardly daring to breathe I followed the old man. Before we had gone ten metres a boy came bounding up. He was about thirteen, degenerate-looking, with the face of a toad and lips covered with horrible sores.

"Please shave me! The beard itches me..." he begged piteously.

"Clear off! Be off with you!" Dementich waved him away.

We passed people dancing, singing, howling, naked and half-naked. One was pretending to be a raven: squatting in a corner he croaked and flapped his arms. Another howled like a wolf. A third searched feverishly in the hair of a fourth. Among these wretches, I saw a familiar face: it was the ex-pilot I had come across the first evening in the bath-house.

An unshaven, emaciated man rushed at me; burning lynx-like eyes stared at me through a mane of matted hair. He clutched a broom which he aimed at my chest.

"Bang, bang! Lie down, you're dead!" he yelled fiercely. Dementich drove him off too. Frankly, I breathed a sigh of relief when we reached the doors which led out of this hell.

The Insulin Ward was below ground, next to the laboratory where Loza and some medical researchers carried out their experiments. On the door hung a sign: "No Entry except for Authorized Personnel. Medical Staff Only".

"We mustn't be long, or they might catch us," whispered Dementich.

In the doorway I stopped. It was a large dimly lit room and from every corner came groans.

"Over here."

We went over to one of the beds. Sasha was lying there, bound hand and foot. Saliva trickled from his open mouth, and the palate was a strange whitish colour. His body trembled in weak convulsions, his eyes were open but the pupils were dull.

"Have they poisoned him?" I stepped back in horror. "Why is the inside of his mouth all white like that?"

"No, that's normal. He's in shock." The old man rubbed his nose and wiped his eyes on the corner of his smock. "Let's go. He's a good lad, that," Dementich shook his head once we were out of the ward. "Well brought up. Always proper with his words, he was. Not like them others, nothing but swearing and blaspheming. They're killing him alive. It's all that Loza and Petters, damned fascists, heathens."

That night I was tormented by dreadful nightmares. I dreamt of a huge bed with a row of naked snarling, groaning, singing men of all ages, all unshaven and filthy. Then I was hugging Vera.

"I like your hair and your grey eyes," she was whispering. "You're strong and you're handsome..."

"Think so, sweetheart?"

"Don't call me that, call me Vera. Why do you always hide behind a mask. Why do you act rough and common and pretend to be crude with women? I know you're not really like that. I want you to be yourself."

136

"You wouldn't understand, but if you want to know, it's best for me that way. I decided to live like that. Anyway, what do you want from me? Whitley is more your type; he's what you need and he really goes for you."

"I don't want him, I want you. I don't like him, I want to be with you. Let's talk about you..."

"I don't like talking about myself. You have a wonderful body, specially your legs and your breasts, particularly your legs..."

I laughed in her face and suddenly saw Sasha.

"Sasha, you're alive! That's great! Let's get away from here."

"No, Bob, I died. I died long ago. I give you my violin..."

His eyes rolled back in their sockets and his body convulsed. I held him, trying to ease his torment and then saw that it wasn't Sasha at all but the Prophet, the loathsome old man who'd attacked the young cleaning woman. The Prophet gripped my shoulders and began to shake me. I jerked awake to find that strong hands were dragging me out of bed...

16

"What time is it, Julia?"

"Three o'clock, Arthur."

"Hmmm," murmured Loza and came up to me. "We've still got time. So how about it, are we going to talk, Parkin?"

So his name was Arthur... What a noble name — King Arthur, the legendary hero — I screwed my eyes up as Loza loosed a cloud of smoke into my face.

It was about half past two in the morning when two orderlies I had never seen before dragged me, still half asleep, out of bed. Now I was standing before him in the middle of the room, squinting against the glare of the lamp directed right into my face. At a table opposite sat Julia Petters, watching me. Behind a screen Vera Cabot was busy with bottles and glasses. I had caught a glimpse of her when they had brought me in, but since then she had kept away from me. Only once had I intercepted a glance full of fury and hatred. I still didn't know what was happening, but I sensed there was nothing good in store. Loza was up to some game, asking meaningless questions such as how I felt, how my friends were — he meant Max and Rolf — what they thought about getting out of here, how well I played football and what had we all thought about the film they had shown after the match. Mention of the film made me cautious. Was it just idle chatter, or ... was it connected with Rakoff's *suicide* while the film was on? If it had to do with Rakoff, then Simon had already betrayed us.

Loza paced about the office talking about his life. Well, it wasn't for that the old fox had dragged me out of bed in the middle of the night. I shifted from one foot to the other. Quick as a flash, Loza turned on me.

"Tired of standing are you? Well, you can go back to your ward and sleep, if..." he paused, "if you tell me who killed Rakoff?"

My fears were justified; Simon had betrayed us. Rolf and Max must be already under arrest.

"Was he killed, then?" I asked innocently.

"Drop it, Parkin! We know everything."

As naturally as I could, I shrugged.

"Why are you asking me?"

"Why you?" he suddenly bellowed. "Is this yours?"

He rushed up and put something on the table, but the light was so blinding I couldn't see what it was.

"I can't see from here, it's the light..."

"Come over here."

I stepped over to the table and saw Lika's ring. I reached out to pick it up, but Loza chopped my hand away.

"Get back to your place! So, it's yours?"

"Yes, it is."

He picked up the ring and slowly read out: "To Boris Henry James from Lika."

Behind the screen Cabot laughed.

"Who's this Henry James? James Bond, or somebody? Acting the James Bond for your Lika, were you? And who's Lika?" He left the table and came right up to me. "So who's Lika, Henry James? Tell us, we're most interested..."

"Yes, Parkin, tell us. We're interested in spy stories, too," chimed in Petters, who until then had taken no part in the conversation.

"Well, Parkin, are you going to talk?" Loza lit another cigarette. "Silence, is it? Well, we know who Lika is — one of your whores..."

I swung and hit him on the jaw, sending him flying back against the opposite wall. After that the orderlies tied my hands behind my back and punched hell out of me for a good ten minutes until I couldn't feel any more. Loza had picked himself up and stood watching the scene in silence. He was all red in the face, now and then wiping the sweat off with handkerchief. Soon I was standing before him again.

"Now you'll be more ready to talk, won't you? Right, let's get to the point," he said as confidently as though I had already agreed to talk.

"When did you lose the ring?"

"Yesterday lunchtime."

"Yesterday? Or was it the day before, at the film show?"

"Yesterday."

"Vera, when did you find it?"

Cabot emerged from behind the screen.

"Right after we found Rakoff had hanged himself. I mean, had been hanged."

Oh Christ, I thought, I must have lost the ring in the corridor when they were tying my hands. She'd found it and, furious that I'd rejected her, had given Loza the ring. Now they believed I'd done the bastard in.

"Hear that? Was it you that hanged him? Who helped you? You couldn't have managed it alone."

"I don't know what you're talking about."

"Listen, lad, don't try and fool me. We don't have too much time. I know you did it, I want to know who helped you?"

"Whitley and Hartmann, of course," said Cabot.

Well, without a qualm she was prepared to shop two of her lovers and send them off to prison.

"Shut up, I know that. I want him to tell it me himself."

I made up my mind to say nothing. They wouldn't squeeze a word out of me about my friends.

"Listen, I advise you to talk." He came up to me again, though not so close this time. "I have the means to make you talk, but I don't want to use them unless I have to. I appeal to your common sense. Now, I'll give you thirty minutes to think it over. Your last thirty minutes. Meanwhile we'll have ourselves a drink and a bite to eat. Get the glasses, girl."

Cabot laid out on the table slices of bread spread with caviar, smoked sturgeon and sliced Cracow sausage, while Loza fetched a bottle of vodka from his desk. Soon they were drinking and stuffing themselves in front of me. Loza put his feet up on the table and downed glass after glass, eating very sparingly. He even invited the orderlies to join in.

For ten days now I'd seen no normal food, let alone caviar sandwiches and spirits. I turned away and scrutinized the walls and ceiling, then switched to the darkly gleaming parquet floor which reflected their shapes. From all around came the sound of crunching and munching — and the aroma! Loza was threatening to force me to tell on my mates. In these ten days I had grown weaker, of course, but I still didn't feel too bad. We'd see who'd win!

Finally they finished.

"Made up your mind to talk?" Loza asked, wiping his greasy mouth with the back of his fist.

"Boris, there's no use staying silent," Cabot came up to me. "Tell Arthur. He'll get it out of you, anyway. And who's this Lika?"

"Whore," I said distinctly.

She recoiled violently.

"You bastard!" she hissed. "I always said he was a bastard. We ought to give him a real good dose. Arthur, dear, let me pump a couple of cc's into him."

Loza laughed.

141

"But wasn't he right, girl?" He put one hand on her breast and pulled her down onto his lap with the other. He was quite drunk.

"Come here and calm down, I know you've always got an itch down there," he patted her in the crotch, "I just didn't know you screwed the patients. So you've been betraying your old cock with this healthy young bull, have you? Not that I'm offended, mind you. Anyway, we've no time to go into that now. You go and get things ready. I'll give it to him myself... Lay him on the couch," he told the orderlies and shook Cabot roughly from his lap.

I resisted but, with my hands and legs tied, they had me stretched out. Soon I was trussed like Sasha yesterday.

"I'm asking you for the last time, was it Whitley and Hartmann who helped you?" He leant over me; his cold eyes had a sinister glint.

There was nothing else for it — I spat right into his face.

He fished out a snowy white handkerchief and proceeded to mop himself dry.

"Vera, bring some caffeine. Is the medinal ready?"

In turn they injected me with both substances and soon I lost all sense of reality. I could see their faces, and I think I must have been laughing wildly because Cabot had long hairs on her upper lip, and on her cheek a carefully cosmetized wart I had never noticed before. Petters wore a wig, which was lop-sided, Loza was all red; sweat poured down his face when he held the syringe. The orderlies were no longer needed and had been sent away.

My tongue loosened and a fit of wild merriment came

over me. I told them all the details, laughing wildly all the time. This quite scared Petters.

"I think you've pumped too much into him, Arthur," she said. "Suppose something happens..."

"What could happen?" I asked happily, lying there with no strength to move a finger. "I feel great! I've never felt better in my whole life..."

"You can go, Julia. I won't need you any more," I heard.

Then there was a complete gap. I don't know how long it lasted, but I came to to the sound of voices — Loza's and somebody else's, higher-pitched. The other person was crying or begging, or something. Consciousness returned slowly until at last I understood what the conversation was about.

"So Parkin had nothing to do with it?" asked Loza angrily.

"Nothing at all," replied the tearful voice. I recognized it now, it was Simon's.

"They tied him up, see. He was trying to stop them. I daren't let out a peep, 'cos they swore they'd kill me too."

"Hmm," murmured Loza. "So that's how it was... And I didn't believe him. All right, Simon. Get back to your ward..."

"No, no!" begged the plumber. "They'll kill me, like they did Rakoff. Put me somewhere else, anywhere — the Violent Wing, please. But I won't go back there."

"What are you blabbering about? Who'll kill you? We've already got Whitley. Well, if you want to move to another department, you can."

I realized they had left. I found that my arms and

143

legs had been untied and tried to sit up, but I couldn't. My whole body felt weighted down and there were circles swimming in front of my eyes. After that I must have lost consciousness again. I remember surfacing and dropping off several times until I heard Loza's voice, muffled as though through cotton wool.

"When he comes to, put him in Thirty-Second Department. No point keeping him in Thirty-Ninth any more. I'm off to bed, girl."

I slipped away again, coming to several times until I awoke at last to the feel of hands touching my body. I was dreadfully weak but I could open my eyes. Maybe I was imagining it, because I saw Vera. She was unbuttoning my pyjama jacket. When she saw me watching her, she hugged me.

"So, Lika's dead. Darling, I'm terribly sorry about your girl. Will you forgive me? Please... I didn't want to do it, he made me. I love you so! Don't you want me?"

In addition to Max and Rolf she was sleeping with Loza — the thought ran faintly through my mind, but my tongue had words of its own.

"Of course I want you..."

"Kiss me, then..."

Through a mist I sought her lips, breathing the fragrance of this unknown body. It was no dream — I could feel her hands roving over me. She did what she wished with me and, hearing her ardent whispers, I felt myself submitting. All thoughts of Max, Rolf and Loza fled from my mind. Afterwards I slipped back into oblivion.

"Wake up, son! Wake up!"

I opened my eyes. Dementich was standing over me, shaking me with his old hands. Tears were running down his face.

"What's the matter?"

"Get up, quick. The dwarf's poisoned himself!" He handed me a sheet of paper.

"I'm to blame for everything. Goodbye, Bob," I read. I sat up in bed.

"Where is he?"

"Lying in the Treatment Room."

"Why is there nobody here?"

"It's one o'clock. They're all at lunch."

"God, I must have slept till one!"

"They gave us orders not to touch you, the murdering swine!"

It was no dream then, what had happened to me the night before. The old man told me — though I knew it now for myself — that under the influence of the antirepressant drugs I had told them the whole story. I'd betrayed everyone. Acting on this, they'd fetched Simon, and he'd saved me — not out of sympathy but for fear the others would kill him. Whitley had been taken away that same night. So far Rolf had not been touched, but he was expecting arrest any moment.

"They took him away from the hospital, our Max," the old man's voice was trembling. "The pock-marked orderly told me he'd seen him carted off in a Black Maria. Must have taken him to prison. So it was your lot did for that devil?"

"Yes, it was us, Dementich."

"Well, now I get it. This morning, when he heard they'd taken him away, the dwarf got real upset. Paced around all morning, really missing him. Then he must have sneaked into the laboratory and grabbed some stuff. Jesus Christ, the things that have been going on here! When they found out that bastard'd been done in, they had all the Americans locked up separate. All the others — loonies and sick ones — got split up round the other departments. Musa and the Count are in Thirty-Second.''

In the Treatment Room I sat on the edge of the couch and looked at the poor dwarf. It was the lifeless, flabby face of a tiny old man. He lay there, pale as a sheet, gazing at nothing.

"Robert, why did you do it?"

He gave me a look that made me ashamed I had asked such a question.

He's going to live, he's going to live, our dwarf!'' Dementich burst into the room, all out of breath. "Petters says he's taken the wrong tablets. They won't kill him.''

I took Robert's hand.

"No, Bob, I don't want to live. I don't want to. Lord, why didn't I die? It was all my fault. If I'd only looked properly, Simon would not have betrayed us.'' Bitterly he began to weep.

I realized he knew nothing. And better so. I returned to the ward where I found my friends back from lunch.

17

I was sitting on my bed, waiting for old Dementich and thinking over all that had happened when the door to the ward opened and in came the two orderlies who had dragged me away last night and later beat me up. I took a good look at them: one was really huge, with fiery-red hair and freckles on his face, hands and neck. The other was lean and scrawny, with a completely shaven head.

The ward went silent.

"Hartmann get your things! You're leaving," said the red-haired one.

Rolf began to collect his things. He had a few books and some underwear and he put these in a canvas hold-all. Suddenly Alyosha rushed up and hugged him.

"Rolf, what's the matter? Where are they taking you?"

Rolf stood there motionless.

"Where's he going?" Alyosha turned to the orderlies. "Take me instead..." He threw himself at the red-haired orderly's feet.

The orderly guffawed and kicked Alyosha in the face. Alyosha gave a howl of pain and clutched his eyes with both hands.

"Let's be off!" The red-haired orderly put his hand on Rolf's shoulder.

Without a word Rolf walked towards the exit, the orderlies following close behind. Alyosha picked himself up, and suddenly leapt onto the back of the shaven-headed orderly and began to throttle him. The orderly tried to throw him off his back but Alyosha had got a death grip on his throat, and the orderly was beginning to wheeze and rattle.

"Fucking queer", said the red-haired orderly. Then, we saw a knife in his right hand and, with full force, he plunged it into Alyosha's back.

A look of surprise came over Alyosha's face. His fingers opened, and he slowly began to slip down the orderly's body as if he was hugging him. For a second he sat on the floor, then fell, face down.

The red-haired orderly quietly pulled the knife out of Alyosha's back, cleaned it on his white smock and put it into his pocket.

Two more orderlies appeared. They looked at Alyosha with dull faces. One announced:

"Anymore queers here? Come on, then."

We stood in silence.

"No one. Good. Get back to your beds".

They left taking Alyosha away with them. The shaven-headed orderly followed them massaging his throat. The red-haired orderly led Rolf away.

The ensuing silence was eventually broken by the heavy thud of a falling object. It was me hurling Alyosha's almost completed statuette of Rolf to the floor. That, at least, they wouldn't get their hands on.

Dementich arrived: he already knew what had happened.

"Collect your things. If we get along to Thirty-Second quickly, you'll be in time for lunch", he told me, sniffing and wiping his nose with his fist.

"What's up?"

"I feel sorry for the Kraut and for the artist as well. He was so delicate... I knew about him and not only I...".

I had no things, apart from my watch which I always wore, the notebook with my journal and Lika's ring which I had found back on my finger when I awoke. I asked if we could drop in and say goodbye to Robert.

Robert was in a deep sleep, heavily sedated. I kissed the sleeping dwarf and trailed after the old man. We left the block and made our way down the path. At the turn I looked back for the last time at the American ward. From the outside it was just like an ordinary two-storied building in dirty brick — rather like a kindergarten.

"You know, the fiddler — he died," said Dementich.

Everything in the park instantly became so still I could hear my own heartbeat. I looked at the old man, horrified, trying to fathom what he had told me.

"What do you mean, died? We saw him only yesterday."

"Well, he's dead," the old man repeated dully. "Mistake, see. Instead of four cc's, they gave him eight and he never came out of shock."

"It's just not possible. Yesterday he was alive; we saw him."

"That was yesterday. Today he's dead. The orderlies were drunk and they botched it."

I couldn't bring myself to believe it, I was utterly floored. Why? He was only twenty-two. He'd done nothing. I remembered Sasha — his tall, thin figure, his

149

beautiful hair... No, it couldn't be true. The old man must be off his head, confused.

"You must have made a mistake, Dementich, surely."

"Mistake nothing. They fetched his ma round and moved him out of the Insulin Ward real quick. Put him in the orderlies' smoking room, they did, so his ma wouldn't know what'd happened. Weak heart again, that's what they wrote. The Marxist had a weak heart and so did the fiddler. All straight and proper, all according to the law. No tripping them up."

"What about Alyosha? How'll they explain about him then?"

"Easy. An accident, the criminals did it because he was, you know... If they knew, the criminals would finish him anyway. He wouldn't get out of here alive. So in fact, they'd be telling the truth. Well, life doesn't do you any favours. It's all the work of that Loza, the fascist — he already put the fiddler down for insulin, and now he's given the artist away to the orderlies..."

I felt sick. Those I loved slipped away irrevocably. Life was just one endless deprivation.

There was nobody else in the canteen where Dementich took me, but they gave me something to eat. Actually the food was quite good, and for the first time I ate meat and decent potatoes. They also gave me some fruit salad and some almost palatable coffee. I cheered up at once, felt much better. The revolting taste in my mouth left by the drugs they had pumped into me last night disappeared immediately.

The first person I saw near the block, which contained Thirty-Second Department, was Leon, squatting by the wall and digging a hole in the ground. When he saw me he drew his head into his shoulders and showed not the slightest sign of pleasure.

"Don't you recognize me, Leon? I'm Parkin. We were Americans together."

"I know," he said weakly, continuing to dig.

"I'm in Thirty-Second too, now, so we'll be together."

"Yes, we will."

"What are you doing?"

"Digging a grave."

Lord, what is it this time...

"Who's died, Leon?"

"Ninochka," he replied mournfully and showed me a small paper package.

"Ah, Ninochka," I said with relief. "What happened to her?"

"She got tired of living, so she died." He turned his head and looked at me so intelligently that it gave me the shivers.

Suddenly I noticed a black eye and some bruises on his face.

"What is it, Leon? Did you fall?"

"I didn't," he answered in a very normal voice. "They beat me up when they found out I'd been fooling them."

"Who beat you up?"

"The Americans first, then the orderlies."

I wasn't even surprised. I knew long ago that Leon had been fooling us, but it didn't matter now.

TWELFTH DAY

That the regime in Thirty-Second Department was much more relaxed I noticed immediately. There were only twelve of us in the ward — two alcoholics, one drug addict and two schizophrenics, apart from me and Leon. The rest were common criminals, real thugs in for the third or fourth time for minor crimes such as drunken brawls or attempted rape. The Count and the Tartar whom they had moved here before me, ran the ward, which echoed to a constant din of shouts and swearwords. Even their conversation, when they were not busy with their crude decks of home-made cards, was of the most basic kind — about women and their merits in bed.

I noticed that they had normal windows here, of ordinary glass, and the top sections were open all day. Not that this was necessary, for there was only one old loony stuck in the ward. In the morning the rest went off to the workshops and after lunch some would go off to work in the gardens while others read in the library, a surprisingly good one for such a God-forsaken dump. The rest of the patients would sit around watching TV in the Recreation Room. Also the people here wore their own clothes and on the way over old Dementich had promised to fetch me mine from the American Ward. This really bucked me up; I was utterly sick of walking around in these striped baggy pyjamas.

It must have been about seven in the evening when I left the library and decided to take a stroll in the park before supper. It was growing cold and dark outside, dusk was gathering rapidly, and after one or two short rain showers it looked as though we were in for a storm. I loved nature like this, on the brink of a great deluge, a storm, for then people usually take to their burrows and that really suited me. It fitted my mood, which was for solitude in this dank, cold garden. I needed to think about myself and all that had happened. There was plenty to think about.

After a while I came upon a large building with a sign on the door: "Occupational Therapy Workshops". The building was in the far corner of the park and seemed new. I walked round it and at the back saw another door with a small sign: "Showers. Staff only".

I went back to the main entrance and tried the door handle. The door was not locked and I went in. There was nobody in the building. It was a huge hall, some 12 metres high, very much like a greenhouse for raising vegetables and flowers. This edifice was all of glass and aluminium supported on several thick wooden pillars. One part of the hall was occupied by long tables, about 4 metres in length, with benches and stools ranged along each side, but most of the room was filled with finished goods. Held back by a network fence were gaudy flowers — red, white, yellow and purple on long stalks of wire wrapped in green paper. They lay on the floor in mounds, waiting to be packed into the large boxes stacked neatly in one corner. The flowers were beautiful, but they struck me as somehow dead. They probably made them for cemeteries, I thought, as I walked gingerly round this flowery grave.

I was standing by the open window, inhaling the fresh scent of real flowers and some strange herbs, when I heard a rustle in the shrubbery outside. Must be a cat, I thought — I had seen a lot of them around the hospital — but it turned out to be a squirrel. The squirrel hopped out onto the path by the window and sat back on its haunches nibbling something. It was small and russet with a huge bushy tail. How on earth did it get here, I wondered, and stood quite still, afraid of scaring this marvellous creature away. At that moment something fell behind me. The squirrel at once vanished into the bushes and I felt a deadly grip on my throat. I couldn't move at all, and then a familiar voice said: "Drag him over here!" I recognized the Count. Swiftly the Count and the Tartar tied my hands and legs with twine and propped me against one of the pillars.

"Well, man, we meet again." The Count's face split by a grin. "We've got some debts to settle — from way back, remember the knuckleduster, and a new one, for Rakoff. He was a good lad."

After this intro he hit me on the jaw, then in the belly,

on the jaw again and after that all over. He ran out of strength at last and Musa took over until he, too, grew tired. After a short rest they hauled me over to one of the tables, spreadeagled me right at one end and lashed me securely to the table top.

"Now say your prayers, and say them loud — I'm a bit deaf," sneered the Count.

I said nothing.

"Can't seem to hear you praying, you creep. We don't have all that much time, somebody might come any minute, so say your goodbyes."

"Come a bit closer, then," I demanded. "A bit more. Right, bend over."

He bent over my face.

"Where'd you get your nose broken, Count?" I asked, quite out of the blue, even with a trace of concern.

"My nose?" He fingered his proboscis. "Well, it must have been about three years ago. Got it in a bit of a punch-up, see. Why?"

"Bit of a punch-up, was it? Well, next time I hope they break your bloody neck. You'll die like a dog in the gutter."

"Lift him up!" he bellowed hoarsely.

Musa began to lever up the heavy table with me lashed to one end. I realized at once what they had in mind and began to reckon the weight of this press with which the Tartar meant to drive me into the floor. It was enough to flatten me into a pancake. I tugged at my bonds, but it was no use, they were too well tied. Musa raised me bit by bit until the table was upended, with me splayed froglike some 4 metres above the floor. I looked down. The floor was solid concrete.

"Right, let him go!" roared the Count.

I shut my eyes and tensed up, then suddenly felt myself flying backwards in the opposite direction. The table crashed down on its legs and a tremendous commotion erupted nearby.

"Hang on a minute, Bob!"

Amazed, unable to credit my eyes, I saw Leon bending over to untie me. He must have come in, just in the nick of time, and simply flattened Musa; I could see the shattered remains of one of the stools. The Count had fled at once to the furthest end of the hall. And that was how my execution did not take place.

"Careful, they're still around somewhere," yelled Leon as I straightened up. "Watch out!"

I dived for the floor as a knife whizzed over my head and stuck into one of the pillars.

"There he is...". At the next moment I saw a welter of bodies.

Leon had tackled the Count. They thrashed around the floor until they fetched up against the net fence holding back the flowers. Despite his bulk, Leon was first on his feet and hit the Count in the pit of his stomach. The Count jacknifed with a groan, Leon straightened him out with one huge paw and fetched him a dreadful blow to the face with the other. The Count rocketed backwards for several metres, crashed through the fence and vanished into a mound of flowers. And then I saw no more, for Musa had leapt on my back. After a brief struggle, I shook him off and then paid him back everything he had given me until he lay flattened, motionless on the floor. By this time the Count had reeled out from among the flowers. Leon picked him up as though he were a feather and hurled him through the wall of glass. The silence after the last shard of glass tinkled to the floor was almost deafening. Musa was crawling towards the exit and I checked Leon, who wanted to hurl him out the same way the Count had gone.

"Okay. As you wish, Bob. Now let's get out of here."

"Where to?"

"What do you mean where to? Right away."

"You mean escape? They'd pick us up at once, especially me, all beaten up."

"No, they won't. I've got it all worked out. I know people that'll help us, places they'll never find us. If we get stopped I'll say you've been in a drunken fight. You don't know how glad I was when I saw they'd moved you to our ward. I realized we ought to get away together. You don't mean to stay here the rest of your life do you? I decided to get out a long time ago, but I didn't want to go alone. I took a liking to you right away, first time I saw you. Sorry I couldn't let you in on the secret. I'll explain everything later. Well, what are you worried about?"

"There are guards on the gate."

"We're not going through the gate. I know a way through the fence, and it'll be as black as pitch in half an hour with this storm coming up. It's just what we need."

I stood there, indecisive. The idea of escape had never occurred to me, but he was right. Was I to rot in this place? The Commission had left me here, and what chance did I stand of ever getting out legally?

"We don't have much time. Make up your mind quick. Supper's in ten minutes and then they'll lock us in."

"Yes, but how can I go in these?" Still resisting

157

feebly, I pointed to my pyjamas. "I'd be picked up by the first cop we see — drunken fight or not..."

"Quiet! Get down!" he hissed suddenly. We sank into the flowers.

From the door, not the main one, but the one leading to the showers, came the sound of male voices.

"It's the orderlies come to wash," Leon whispered.

We froze. There were three of them. After some banter and laughter they closed the door and we heard the sound of running water. Leon laughed.

"What's so funny?"

"Nothing, it's just that now we can get you a suit."

I got the idea and didn't like it, but Leon had already crept up to the rear door and was beckoning urgently. We stopped by the door. The dressing room was quiet, but from the shower room came singing and laughter mingled with the sound of running water. Very cautiously Leon opened the door a crack. Clothes lay on the benches.

"Grab some quick!"

I snatched the nearest bundle and Leon dashed out of the building with me limping after him. It was already half dark, I could see almost nothing, and I followed him by the rustle of twigs as he pushed through the undergrowth.

"Over here!" he hissed.

We veered off through another section of the shrubbery until we came up against a thick, continuous hedge.

"We've got to crawl through it, and it's damned thorny the buggers!" He dived right in.

I followed. Thoroughly scratched by the thorns, we emerged on the other side by a high wooden fence.

"Over here. We've got to count off exactly one hundred

and three planks." He set off along the fence.

I could hear him counting: "One, two, three... ninety-one, ninety-two... a hundred and three."

"Ah, here it is!"

I could see nothing, but I heard him prising back one of the already damaged planks.

18

A moment later and we were on the other side. There was about a hundred and fifty metres of open ground between us and a small wood, and the ten minutes it took to cross seemed the longest in my entire life. If the weather hadn't suddenly changed, we would have been in plain view of the guards at the gate, which was situated on a small hillock.

At last we reached the wood. From the carpet of rotting leaves came a thick, dank smell and I greedily inhaled the pure forest air. Joyfully I snorted like a young colt.

"What the hell are you doing?" growled Leon. "Come on, we've got to get a move on. And change those clothes. You can't go on the road looking like that."

He was right, of course. Painful though it was I slipped off the hated pyjamas and struggled into my stolen suit, not forgetting to transfer my diary. The suit was too small for me. I felt the bottoms of my trousers; they didn't even reach my ankles, and as I bent to check them, the jacket split down the back. Still, beggars can't be choosers.

"Where shall I put these rags?" I said waving them in the dark.

"Up your arse if you like. Give it here. I'll bury them in the wood."

He took the bundle from me and we continued into the darkness. It was only then I realized that in our haste I'd forgotten to grab any shoes. Stupid, stealing a suit and forgetting the shoes. My wretched slippers were already soaked from the dew.

"I didn't get any fucking shoes."

"What?"

"I forgot the shoes. All I've got is my slippers."

"Oh, come on! I'll get you some shoes tomorrow. We'll be out of the wood in a minute and it'll be nice and dry on the main road."

For a few minutes more we proceeded in silence and I thought how good it was — this path, the dark trees and beyond them the cars tearing along the road. After so many days locked in with the stench and the fug everything seemed so wonderful that it was almost like a physical pain. I gave no more thought to shoes and tried to forget my bruises. Soon we had crossed the wood and through the last row of trees we could see lights. We'd reached the road. We must be about 30 kilometres from Moscow and ten from the motorway.

"Wait, I'll go and see whether there's anybody down there..."

He left me and began to pick his way down to the road. I leaned against a tree savouring the smell of the pines. Never had it seemed so marvellous. Suddenly, on the right, something large and black came looming towards me. I slipped to one side in the darkness. Lord, what's this? It was a cow! But how had it got here? The cow came on, gently chewing away, and I went up and put my arms round its neck. A passing headlight drew a gleam from its eye. The cow looked at me, surprised, licked me with its rough tongue and said nothing. Regretfully I let go and the cow lumbered off.

"Bob, where are you?"

"Over here."

"There's nobody on the road. Wait a moment while I bury your things."

I could hear him scraping away the grass and moss from under a tree.

"Right, that's it. You're not an American any more..."

Laughing, we negotiated our way down the steep bank and emerged on to the road. At once a fit of mad merriment overcame me.

"I'm free! Hurrah! Ha-ha-ha!" I shouted with all my might.

"Cut it out! We've still got to get to Moscow, then you can celebrate."

I paid no attention, but grabbed a litter bin and overturned it in the middle of the road. I tossed pebbles into the air, tried to dance (with difficulty due to the beating the Count and Musa had given me) and I felt like a ten-year-old boy at last let out for a walk after some long illness. Then I started to sing.

"You crazy idiot, shut up! Somebody's coming. Over there." He tugged at my sleeve.

I stopped immediately and saw something moving ahead. As we drew closer we made out an old woman, all in black, hobbling along the road with a bag of sticks on her back.

"Let's give you a hand, grandma," I offered.

The old woman shied away in horror and darted down

a path into the wood muttering:

"Keep off me, you devils! Satan begone!"

She vanished into the darkness. For ten minutes or so after that we walked on without seeing a soul. Not a single car passed us.

"When we get to the motorway, we'll hitch a lift."

"We don't have any money," I pointed out.

"Oh yes we do. Two hundred roubles. I've had that smuggled in to me by a friend." He patted the inside pocket of his jacket. "Enough to get us down to the Caucasus, and they'll never catch us there. I've got friends all over. All we've got to do is get down there."

Leon happened to be a Georgian Jew and an actor, apparently quite a talented one, which would explain why he had managed so successfully to fool us and the doctors for so long. He had lived and worked quietly in Tbilisi, the capital of Georgia, until one day someone told him that all the Jews in Moscow were emigrating to Israel. He made several attempts to get an exit visa but was refused each time. Then someone told him that it was very easy to get out if you were a loony as the authorities didn't like having to take care of loonies and were only too glad of an apportunity to get rid of one. That is why Leon decided to become a loony.

A little way ahead we could see bright lights and a group of people busy at something on the road. Parked nearby was a military lorry.

"Soldiers repairing the road," said Leon. "If they ask, we're off to Moscow to see a sick brother."

But they didn't stop us and we passed by.

"A good thing they didn't stop us or they'd have noticed your slippers and your face all bloody. I bet everybody in the area knows there's a loony bin here."

We were about a hundred metres beyond the road-menders when a small oncoming van with a Moscow number plate pulled up at the side of the road and a short fat man with glasses and a hat got out, waving a map.

"You from hereabouts, boys? I've lost my way. Maybe you know how to get to Nagatino? I've been driving in circles for an hour, just can't find the damned place." He was almost begging us.

"Er, Nagatino..." I mumbled. I knew the way to Nagatino all right. I was going to tell him, when I felt Leon tugging at my sleeve.

"Fraid we're not from round here, mate. You'd best ask the lads working on the road down there. They'll know for sure. Maybe you'll give us a lift to the junction," Leon said.

"I'd better find the way first."

He got out and walked towards the workmen, leaving the car with its engine still running.

"Jump in, quick! No, over there, I can't drive," he yelled and made a dash for the car.

It all happened so quickly I had no time to think or argue. I hurled myself into the driver's seat, slammed the car into gear, spun round and tore away at top speed. In the mirror I could see the fat man running after us and yelling, something I could not hear.

He chased us until he was out of breath.

I'd no time to think of the consequences of what Leon had got me into; I was too busy concentrating on the road, for the rain was making the surface slippery. Leon was half turned, looking back.

"There's a lorry after us."

I looked in the mirror and saw a lorry coming up at

163

full speed.

"Maybe it's not after us," but I speeded up all the same.

"It's that truck with the workmen. And the man who owns the car's with them."

I glanced in the mirror again and saw that he was right. It was the same military lorry that had been parked by the roadside. It had narrowed the gap and I could now see quite clearly a young soldier behind the wheel and next to him another soldier and the fat man, who seemed to be yelling and threatening us with his fist.

I pushed the car faster. Seventy kilometres an hour — it was dangerous to do any more on this wet road, besides the van was very old. I pulled away a little, but then hit a series of bends which slowed us down. Soon the truck reappeared in the mirror. I put my foot down. A road sign flashed past — 8 kilometres to Motorway. Before we reached the junction we could turn off into the wood, ditch the car and hide, later returning to the road and hitching a lift. That was my plan. As soon as this twisting section ended, I could step on the gas. But instead the bends came faster and tighter, and on one we almost slid off into the ditch. I had to reduce speed. The truck slowed down too, but it still came on at a fair pace; it was heavier and didn't skid so easily. Soon they had almost caught us up. The fat man was leaning out of the window and we could hear him yelling:

"Stop, you bastards! We'll get you anyway."

Leon was growing nervous.

"Quicker! Quicker!" he was almost shouting.

I put my foot down again, the needle crept up to eighty once more and we soon pulled away from them.

"Ten minutes more, then turn off into the wood. We can ditch the car and get away on foot."

He had the same idea as I. But then came a sign:

"Reduce Speed. Dangerous Bends. Steep Gradients." We were plainly out of luck. We couldn't abandon the car and escape into the wood in full view of the people in the lorry. This bloody stretch would be over, soon.

The road climbed up and up until the near side fell off into a steep, sandy embankment. The wood petered out, all our plans were ruined. Down below there must be some sort of construction work in progress during the day, for I could see brightly-lit vehicles parked around but no sign of people. I had to slow right down and nurse the car round the bends now, for one slight jerk of the wheel could send us sliding down the slope. The truck reappeared on the horizon and began to catch us up. Soon it was hanging right on our tail. This time the situation was really serious. Fatty was yelling at us to stop and not damage the state-owned car. Suddenly the lorry driver pulled out to the left and began to overtake. He drew level and for a while we drove side by side. Then he swung back to the right, almost grazing our car.

"What the hell's he doing?" yelled Leon, scared.

"What do you think he's doing?" I put my foot down in an effort to pull ahead.

The lorry caught us up again, again swung left and right. This time I felt a slight blow. I couldn't push the car any faster because we were now on a narrow, winding stretch of road with a steep drop to the right. Time and again the truck tried to cut in to us and banging against my offside. Then one enormous crash and the car was hurled over to the right. I stamped on the

165

brakes, but it was too late, we hurtled down over the edge. I remember in the mirror seeing the truck follow us; it too had lost control.

I don't know how much time passed. For a moment after I opened my eyes I didn't know where I was. Something heavy was pressing me down. I tried to move, but I couldn't. Then it all came back. I didn't know whether I was alive or not. Now my brain began to function and I tried to move my arms. That I could do. The weight pressing me down, I found, was Leon sprawled on top of me. Somehow I eased him off. In the dim light of a lamp I could see his mouth gaping open with a thin trickle of blood over one lip. His eyes were staring at me in a sort of guilty smile.

"Leon, are you all right?" I touched his shoulder.

There was no answer. I scrambled out of the wreckage, amazed that my arms and legs were intact, that I was alive. I tried to drag Leon out of the car, but it was impossible; the lower half of his body was sandwiched between the engine and the dashboard. Without special cutting equipment there was no way of getting him out. I leant over, ripped open his shirt and listened for a heartbeat. Nothing, and his hands were strangely cold. I straightened up, realizing with horror that Leon, who for those few hours had become the person closest to me, was dead. The realization sent me charging away from the wreck. At some distance I turned and saw smoke rising.

19

Pushing through a thicket I came upon a metal fence about twice the height of a man. What was this? Perhaps I could spend the night here and get to Moscow in the morning. I was exhausted. In the darkness I had no idea which way to go, so the best plan would be to find a place to sleep. I followed the fence around to a metal gate with a sign: "Wood Store. Authorized Personnel Only".

Hell, everywhere was restricted, everywhere was out of bounds. After all, I had no intention of taking anything, but if it was dry and I could sleep there, why the hell shouldn't I get in. I looked at the inside. There was a roofed-over area, almost a barn, in which the wood was neatly stacked. It was dimly lit by a single electric bulb; the corners were dark and would surely be dry. Then I noticed a bicycle. God, what a chance! It was just what I needed. I could get some sleep in the corner, under the roof, and take off on the bicycle in the morning. I would leave it near a police station with a note for it to be returned to its owner. I tried the gate. It was open. Encouraged, I entered the yard. Now I could get my head down. In a corner of the roofed-in area stood a wooden table and on it a God send — an open bottle of milk and some potatoes. Real jacket potatoes — three whole potatoes! A tremendous hunger overcame me. After all, I'd had nothing since lunch. I stuffed one potato into my mouth and swallowed it down with barely a bite. Then I reached for the bottle of milk and took a huge swallow. With the last gulp something like a snarling tiger landed in the middle of my back. The impact knocked me to the ground but I rolled over immediately and came face to face with an Alsatian guard dog. I kicked it off but it attacked again. We rolled around on the earth floor and I felt its fangs snap near my throat. It was on my chest and I gathered all my strength to throw it off. It snarled and tore at my clothes and skin. There was something hard digging into my ribs and I realized we had rolled onto the logs. Kicking the dog away from me I snatched up a log and as it leapt back I battered it over the head. It yelped and loosed its hold on my shoulder. Again and again I pounded it with the log. Once again it howled, then went still and slumped to the floor, while I continued to beat and beat at it in my fury. My strength spent, I tossed the log, covered in blood, to one-side. I looked at the dog with bitterness and revulsion. It was a large, beautiful bitch, still young. I turned away from the sight. I loved dogs and would never have touched it if it had not attacked me.

The wood store was quiet at last and I could have finished off the potatoes and milk and got some sleep in a corner behind the logs, but the place sickened me now and I left. By some miracle I came out on the road just by a signpost: Moscow, 12 kilometres. I set off along the verge. The rain became heavier and it was only now I noticed there was also a wound in my leg. I reached down and found that the dog must have bitten through a ligament, but in the heat of battle I had felt nothing. My wounded shoulder also ached as well as the rest of my body. I limped along in my slippers, now completely soaked.

After a while I heard the sound of an approaching car. I didn't bother to look back, for I had no intention of trying to hitch a lift. I'd had enough of cars. It was a bus, quite empty. The driver, a young lad, stopped of his own accord.

"If you're going to Moscow, jump in, mate. I'll give you a lift, " he offered.

With difficulty I clambered up into the cab.

"I'm on my way back to the depot," he said. "Got soaked, did you?"

I nodded.

"Hang on a bit, I'll switch on the heating. You'll be warm soon."

He pulled a switch and a blast of hot air enveloped my legs and then my whole body.

"That better, then?"

"Fine, thanks."

"Where are you from so late?"

I wasn't in the mood for talking but I had to tell him something.

"Been visiting my woman. Got held up fighting her husband and missed the last bus..."

"And the wife's sitting up for you at home," grinned the driver. "We'll be in the centre in about forty minutes. The depot's near the Zoo. That do you?"

"Well, if you can drop me off at the station. It's closer for me."

We made good time and soon reached the station square. I climbed down from the cab and thanked him. The big clock in the square showed eleven twenty-five.

THIRTEENTH DAY

I decided to go into the buffet. I had no money; I just wanted to sit and think what to do next.

I went into the hall and sat down at an empty table trying to hide my face. A drink would have been a godsend, for I was soaked to the skin. I remembered Leon had said he had two hundred roubles. Why the hell hadn't I taken them. They would really have come in useful now.

At the next table sat a character with a briefcase and I noticed him eyeing my split and torn jacket and my general appalling state. Just the sort to go and report me, I thought anxiously. But just then a fat, heavily made-up woman rushed by, dragging along a plump, but very pretty little girl.

"You idiot! You fool!" cried the woman. "Our train's going and he sits here drinking." She turned and rushed for the exit, hauling the girl after her. The man with the briefcase trotted after her, barely able to keep up.

I sighed with relief. Suddenly I felt cold. Outside the freezing rain was pouring down. I began to shiver, must have caught a chill. I thrust my hands in my jacket pockets to warm them up and felt some paper in one of them. It was two crumpled rouble notes. Lord, a whole two roubles! Untold wealth! The list of my crimes was lengthening every moment! Now I had stolen a jacket with two roubles. As soon as I could I would get it cleaned and mended and post it back to the hospital along with two roubles. The thought calmed me a little. I must think what to do next, but first I needed a drink.

"What do you want, then?" asked a fat waitress, attracted by my wave and staring at my face.

"Double measure of vodka."

At the next table sat a grubby man with matted hair and a several day's growth of beard. He was served a steak. A beautiful looking collie laid her fine muzzle on his lap. The man ate with his fingers, pulling pieces off the steak. He was almost toothless, I noticed. From time to time he would extract a piece of meat from his mouth and toss it to the collie.

My waitress returned with a small decanter of vodka and glass on a damp battered tray. But before I even had time to pick up the carafe I heard a voice behind me:

"Stand us a vodka, darling?"

I turned round. Near me stood a woman, aged about 35, with a round, very beautiful face. She was wearing a good grey costume and a matching beret. There was no doubt as to her trade. I beckoned to the waitress again.

"What is it this time?" asked the waitress, annoyed.

"Another glass, and a clean one, please."

The woman asked me if she might sit down. The glass

171

arrived and I poured her a shot of vodka.

"Your good health, gorgeous," she said with slight irony looking at my battered face.

She downed the vodka at one go, took a silk handkerchief from her leather bag and wiped her lips. Then she took out a packet of cheap cigarettes.

"Like one?"

I took a cigarette, struck a match and lit up for us both.

"I live near here. Want to come?"

I took a long pull on my cigarette as I looked at her closely. A handsome woman, healthy looking, peaches and cream complexion, from the country to judge by her accent.

"Thanks, but I've got to see someone."

I stood up and laid a rouble on the table.

"As you wish," she said with a trace of regret and stood up too. "If you need a place for the night, I'm always here."

"Thanks, but I doubt it."

I left her and went to the exit. So far I had been lucky, except for the filthy weather. The rain had now been joined by a fierce, cold wind. I decided I'd go along and see my friend Dan. He had a large apartment and maybe I could get a few hours sleep and a wash and think over what to do next. Once again I felt terrible.

Dan lived not far from the station. The shape I was in I couldn't take a bus or a tube. I had one rouble left, and I took a taxi.

The driver, too, looked askance at my face and tattered jacket, and again I was worried that he might phone in and report me. I kept an eye on the meter and as soon as it registered 75 copecks I stopped the taxi. I gave the driver a 15 copeck tip, which left me with ten.

It was twenty minutes past twelve by the time I got to Dan's and rang the bell. He answered the door himself, sleepy-eyed and groggy.

"Ah, it's you!" he said looking startled at the state of my face but with no trace of surprise at my arrival as though we had seen one another only yesterday.

"Come in, but be quiet or you'll wake the kid."

We went into his study and I gave him a quick rundown of all that had happened.

"I know, old boy. The whole of Moscow knows. The bush telegraph just didn't know the end of the story," he muttered, still half asleep. "Want something to drink? I think I've got something."

"Well, I wouldn't say no."

"Let's go in the kitchen."

In the kitchen he took a bottle from the refrigerator. It was cheap table wine.

"Don't you have anything stronger?"

"That's all, there's nothing else."

I broke the seal, and filled the glass with the dark, cherry-coloured liquid. It tasted dreadful, but then beggars can't be choosers.

"Do you have any bread and sausage?"

"Yes, over there. Help yourself."

He sat on a stool, dully watching me eat and drink and then began to trim his toenails with a pair of large sewing scissors.

"Maybe I'll have a drink with you."

I poured him out the rest and explained that I needed somewhere to stay for a few days while I planned what to do. The wine seemed to bring him to at last and he was horrified to learn that I had escaped from the hospital.

"God, man, they'll pick you up straight away. They're probably on your trail already. Listen, they know about us, they know we're friends, so they'll be coming round here. I'm sorry but... I have a family. I must think of my wife and child."

"All right, I'll go. Thanks for the wine and the food." I got up and went towards the door. In the doorway I turned. "Oh, maybe you'd give me some shoes till tomorrow. You can see what I'm wearing."

"Yes, of course," he agreed eagerly. "That I can do."

As quickly and as quietly as he could he went into the next room and rummaged around for some time before returning with a pair of sandals.

Good grief, it's pouring with rain and the man gives me sandals!

"Here you are, I'm afraid that'll all there is. Look, I'm sorry."

I took the sandals — they were better than the wretched slippers and, the main thing, more like normal footwear.

20

I went out into the street. The rain showed no intention of abating and the wind was stronger than ever. I dropped the slippers in a litter bin and walked on, not really clear where I was going. As I'd thought, within ten minutes Dan's sandals were completely soaked.

Suddenly I recalled that Max's mother lived near here.

She'd take me in! That was a stroke of luck! And I had good reason to call, for I had to tell her what had happened to Max and Rolf; I doubt whether she already knew. We had met once; Max had introduced me on one of her visits to the hospital and I think she'd taken a liking to me. I recalled her — a youngish, attractive and successful woman. She'd never leave me out in the street. I walked quickly and soon, in the light of a swinging, wind-blown street lamp saw the number of her house. By this time I was soaked to the skin again.

I rang the doorbell. Nobody answered. I rang again. Nothing. Then the door of the next flat opened and a head bristling with curlers emerged.

"She's not there."

"You wouldn't know when she'll be back?"

"She's not coming back," said the head. "She's moved."

"Perhaps you know her new address?"

"I don't know and I don't want to know, and you'd better push off quick, too."

The head withdrew and the door slammed to. I went downstairs. Outside nothing had changed. The rain beat in my face as I walked and the wind cut through my skin like a razor. After a while I had no strength left. My watch had stopped and I had lost all sense of time. I took shelter in the doorway of a very smart residential house and tried to warm myself up a bit, but there was an awful draught and I decided I'd be better up on the top floor where it would be warmer.

On the top landing there was only one flat and opposite the door, against the wall, a radiator. The radiator was warm and I huddled against it as a man might cuddle up to his girl. How long I sat there I don't know; I must have dozed off, for what woke me was the slam of the main door downstairs and the sound of voices and laughter. I turned nervously and opened my eyes. This was a smart, respectable house and my tattered figure did not go with this imposing entrance, marble stairs and deep pile carpets: if anyone saw me here, they'd ring for the police at once. After all I'd gone through I'd no intention of being caught.

I struggled to my feet and started down the stairs. On the second-floor landing I came upon a couple — a man in a felt hat and light overcoat, and a heavily made up woman in a silk raincoat. When they saw me, they stopped laughing and stared at me suspiciously. Studiously ignoring them, I hurried down the stairs as fast as I could manage.

Outside it was still cold, and raining cats and dogs. I couldn't go back to my own flat. In the first place I didn't have my keys — they were back in the hospital — and I would have roused the neighbourhood if I'd tried to break in at night. Anyway the police would be watching the flat hoping to pick me up. Still, I'd have to think of something, perhaps get somebody to go over and pick up some clothes and money, especially money. Without that I couldn't move. But what should I do now? I decided to go back to the station; at least it would be warm and dry there. Now I had some normal footwear — if not suited for this wretched weather, at least it was normal, not hospital slippers, but I'd have to keep away from the police. I must be very careful.

Somehow I found my way to the station. It was warm and crowded. In the main waiting room some oriental-looking types with crates and boxes were chattering away loudly in their own language. Clutching their bundles, women lay side by side with their dirty, snotty-nosed kids on the filthy, spittle-spattered floor. A young soldier was sitting on a bench rolling a cigarette.

I found myself a dark place by a wall. For a while I sat up and tried to appear as though I were waiting for a train too. My eyes kept closing, but I fought off sleep; I didn't want to drop off in front of everyone; I was afraid the police would come round. I'd heard a lot about police checks at the stations. Mostly they were looking for prostitutes, but they rounded up anybody who seemed suspicious. Still, for the time being there was no sign of them. From time to time porters would appear in their white aprons announcing the arrival or departure of a train, shouting above the loudspeakers and offering their services. Each time their yells made me shudder.

I was cold and miserable. I turned up my jacket collar and slumped against the wall. For a number of nights I had slept badly, I'd eaten poorly, and the tension of those days, together with my fever and the beating up was beginning to break me down. I kept a grip on myself and somehow managed to keep awake, mainly because of a peasant next to me. On a large handkerchief he had set out bread, an onion, salted gherkins, hard-boiled eggs and sausage. He ate noisily, washing down the food with beer from the bottle. I couldn't keep my eyes off his food. A sandwich, a glass of cheap wine and a shot of vodka was all I'd had. At last the peasant finished his meal: neatly he shook the crumbs from his handkerchief into his mouth, wiped his lips with the back of his hand and left. I dozed off.

I woke to find somebody tugging at my sleeve. I jerked nervously and opened my eyes. At first I was afraid it might be the police and they would take me back to that place, but no — it was the woman in the grey costume and beret I had treated to vodka a couple of hours ago.

"It's you, you've come back. What are you doing around here? Cor, you're all soaked." She put a hand on my forehead. "And you've got a fever. Listen, let's go to my place. I'll fix you some tea and hot wine. You can lie-down and then go your way. I don't want anything from you."

She pulled me to my feet. Now I didn't care, I had difficulty making out what she was saying. Things swam before my eyes, my head felt hot and I was staggering from weakness and fever. To an outsider it would seem as though she were helping a drunken boyfriend.

We went out into the street. The rain was still going strong and we trudged ankle deep in water. She slung my arm around her neck.

"Give me a hug, darling. That's it. Cor, you're heavy," she laughed. "If I wasn't such a strong girl, we'd never make it."

She brought me to the place where she lived and we climbed a creaking wooden staircase to the first floor. It was quite dark on the landing, only the light from a streetlamp coming obliquely through the window dimly lit her generous figure. She propped me up against the wall while she opened her bag.

"It's dark. The bloody caretaker never fixes the light, no matter how much you nag him."

She turned to face me, and in the semi-darkness I could see that she was smiling. At last she found her key, opened the door and switched on the light. It was one largish, very clean room with faded wallpaper. There was a blue cloth lampshade, a plain deal table, two chairs, a chest of drawers with a mirror, a wardrobe and a faded curtain on a string, half screening a wide unmade bed.

She caught me staring at this love couch.

"I'll change all the sheets in a minute."

She tossed her beret on the table, letting her thick black hair free. She went to the chest, opened a drawer and took out some sheets and pillowcases, even a blanket still in its original wrapping.

"There you are, it's all clean, washed it myself. And the blanket's brand new, never been used before. You can sleep there".

"And where are you going to sleep?"

"There's room for both of us, I won't disturb you if I'll doss down here, on the floor."

"It'll be cold, you'll catch a chill."

"Who me? I'm as strong as a horse. It won't bother me a bit."

She pulled off my sopping wet jacket and trousers, slipped off my sandals and sat me down on a chair.

"Jesus Christ, what a state you're in! And what's wrong with your leg and shoulder?"

"A dog attacked me."

From a wall cabinet she fetched some cotton wool, bandages and surgical spirit and began to clean up my wounds. Then she put on cotton wool pads and bound them tightly.

"Your legs are like ice! We had better warm them up. Just as soon as I get the water boiling and also rub you with some vodka. We'll get some tea into you and by morning you'll be fit for any girl." She started rubbing my legs gently with her warm, plump hands.

Then, she went into the kitchen and I could hear the clatter of pots and pans. In a few minutes she was back with a large metal basin from which steam was rising. She set the basin by my feet, squatted down and dipped a towel in the hot water. Then in turn she rested my legs in her lap, wrapped the towel round my foot and carefully massaged my leg. The towel was scalding hot at first, but I soon got used to it. She rubbed and kneaded my deadened toes and feet until I felt the warmth creeping back. Then she laid me on the bed, took the bowl back into the kitchen and returned with a litre bottle of vodka and another towel, a dry one. She held the towel to the top of the bottle and shook it vigorously a few times. At once there was a strong smell of alcohol. She drew back the blanket and began to rub my bruised chest and legs, then turned me over onto my stomach and rubbed my back. I felt the alcohol soak in.

"You're a big bloke! Not bad looking. A few bruises won't bother you. You need some tea and a good night's sleep and you'll be as right as rain in the morning. My husband, when he was alive, I always cured his cold like this. He was too delicate, always catching something. That's how he took and died; nothing anybody could do about it."

With evident pleasure she turned me over again onto my back, slipped on a pair of pyjamas, put some thick wool socks on my feet and wrapped my legs in a woman's woolen cardigan. Then she drew up the blanket and piled more clothes on top of this. I lay there cocooned, almost asleep, but she brought in the kettle and shook me awake. She poured out a mug of hot water, tipped in a quarter of a packet of dried raspberries and two spoonfuls of sugar and raised it to my mouth.

"Keep your hands tucked in, I'll feed it to you. I'm not one of your delicate young misses, you know."

She sat down on the bed, raised the mug and began to feed me like a child, small sips at a time, occasionally wiping my mouth with a clean handkerchief.

"Well, darling, feeling better?" she laughed, displaying even, white teeth. And that's not all, either."

Once again she vanished into the kitchen and was busy so long that I all but dozed off.

"I know you want to sleep, but in a minute. First you've got to drink this. It's the best thing for colds — raises the dead, they say". She held out a glass of hot wine, which I poured down me.

After all these ministrations I was so hot I began to sweat. Slowly I felt life returning to my aching body. After two weeks of nightmares, sleepless nights and tension I slept soundly for the first time.

FOURTEENTH DAY

21

I awoke with the feeling of somebody's presence in the room. It was dark and for a moment I didn't know where I was, what time it was, day or night. Then it all came back. I tried to sit up in bed and at once she murmured.

"Go back to sleep. It's early yet."

"What's the time?"

"Two o'clock."

"Two o'clock?"

"Two o'clock in the morning..." She got up, switched on the table lamp and rested her bare arms on my blanket. "You've slept right round the clock, darling. Get more sleep. It's night again now."

"So that's it! Today must be Thursday. Is it still raining?"

"It's stopped, but it's still damp out."

"I'd best get up." Gingerly I swung my legs out of bed. "I don't suppose you've got a shower?"

"In a dump like this? No, there's no shower. They've been promising to put one in for a year, but they haven't done a damned thing. I haven't got the money to bribe them. Anyway, it doesn't matter — I've got something instead of a shower. I'll go and get it ready."

In one easy motion she got to her feet and stood there in a long white nightgown. Her hair was loose on her shoulders. She had a good, full, peasant's body. Scorning a dressing gown or anything of the sort, she padded barefoot into the kitchen where she was busy for a good twenty minutes. Then her head poked round the door.

"It's all ready, darling. In you come. I've fixed a little bath for you that's as good as any of your showers."

I followed her into the kitchen. It was a small room with neatly painted white walls and ceiling. In one corner was a kitchen table, painted green, and the window was hung with a bright print curtain. On the floor stood a metal tub full of steaming water.

"Am I supposed to wash in that?"

"And what's wrong with it? I always wash in it, and I used to bath my son in it. It's his tub, really. What did you think I used it for, then?" She gave me an offended look. "Nobody else had washed in it. I don't keep a man long; once he's finished, he goes off. I just ask that he leaves the money on the table."

I listened to her with disgust. Then I looked at my new bath. A child's tub! It was too small for me, but I was desperate for a wash. I wanted to wash away all traces of my stay in that nightmarish place and everything else that had happened.

"All right, you go out."

She left. I got undressed and dipped one foot in the tub. The water was very hot. Of course, the tub was too small for me, but after some careful manoeuvring, trying

183

not to wet my bandages I wedged myself in.

"Are you in yet?" came her teasing voice.

"Yes."

She came in with a loofah and a cake of good soap. "Now I'll scrub you," she laughed, soaping my head. When she had worked up a good lather, she rinsed it off with water from the kettle. She repeated this performance three times, lathering and rinsing, then she soaped the loofah and began to scrub away at my back.

"Hey, go easy! It's not the floor you're scrubbing but my back and it's already sore."

"Too hard for you? Well, now you're in there you've got to take it."

She came round to the other side and rubbed away at my chest, then made me stick my feet out and soaped and scrubbed them.

"Now we've got to rinse you off. Come on, stand up! Or are you shy? I won't look. Think I've never seen a naked man before? Stand up when I tell you! I want to rinse you clean."

I stood up with my back to her. She picked up a bucket and drenched me with water.

"Ufff, that's good!" I let out.

"There," she laughed, "what did I tell you? Right, out you get! Step on this."

She pointed to a clean cloth on the floor. I got out, still keeping my back to her. She picked up a bath towel from a stool and wrapped it round me from behind up to my armpits.

"There, you're finished," she said in her soft, throaty voice.

Suddenly I felt her large, plump arms around me. I took hold of her hands and slowly turned to face her.

184

She stood there, head lowered, her hair loose, in her long, white and by now half-soaked nightgown. The thin material clung and moulded itself to her full body. I could see she had strong thighs and full swaying breasts. I put one hand under her chin and raised her face. She looked at me with large, magical eyes, and I saw that she was young and beautiful. I picked her up in my arms — and she was no lightweight — and carried her into the room.

I was really hungry for sex as I had had no woman for the last two months. I thought of Vera Cabot. I had failed with her because I was under drugs, something I began to regret. Now after all this nursing and a good sleep I was strong again. And a beautiful woman wanted me.

She was wonderful and exciting and gave herself not as a whore but as if she really loved me at that moment.

"Would you like a cigarette?"

"Yes."

She reached over to the bedside table and took a pack of cigarettes and a box of matches from the drawer. I took one and inhaled deeply.

"You don't smoke?"

"Yes, but only to be sociable really. I don't like them, they're not very tasty," her eyes gleamed in the half dark.

"And what is tasty?" I puffed out a smoke ring and slipped my arm round her shoulders.

She looked at me teasingly.

"It's not *what*, it's *who*'s tasty."

"All right, who's tasty?"

"You are," she laughed.

"You enjoyed it, then?"

"With you — yes," she bent her head bashfully.

"Where are you from?"

"Oh, a long way away. From the country. I ran away from a village and worked as a domestic help for one of the Party bosses. He'd wanted me to come for a long time. His wife's a bit of an old goat and can't cope with him, if you know what I mean. So he lived with me and we had a son. I took him to my mother's, and here I..." She hesitated. "Don't think I've been doing this for long. Three months, that's all. And I'm not old, either. I'm not thirty-six yet."

"Who got you a room in Moscow if you're from the country?"

"Oh, this Party boss got me a residence permit right off. He's got connections in the police. And when I left him, I got a job with a construction firm and they gave me this dump. Said it'd be knocked down soon anyway, and then I'd get a bed-sitter flat. Then I could really live..."

"So you're a building worker, are you?"

"No, think I'm a fool? As soon as they gave me a room, I packed the job in. Listen, darling, stay here and I'll cook and wash for you, everything you need."

186

"Why me?" You don't even know me?"

"Because I like you. Your eyes look honest to me."

"Thanks, it's very nice of you, but I can't. I've got things to do, and I'd be best off out of Moscow for a bit."

She rested her plump arms on my chest while she thought.

"Got to get away. Have you any where to go?"

"That's the trouble, I don't."

"Ah, darling, well I'll tell you one. Go and stay with my mother. She's a forestry worker, lives in the woods and looks after my little boy. You could stay with her for a bit, and after that it'd be up to you. You'd be quite free to go."

I stroked her hair.

"You are a good sort, but how can I accept an offer like that? Your mother doesn't know me; whatever would she think? No, it's impossible."

"I'd go with you and introduce you, stay a bit myself. Then I'd come back. I have to be here, I've got my mother and the boy to support. But I'd come down on Fridays. My mother's a good sort, she'll do everything for you and she'd be honoured to have you as a guest. She'll be amazed to see an educated type like you; I've never had anybody like that before."

"What sort have you had then?"

"Oh, very humble people like myself." She gave me a strong hug. "Ah, you're a marvel. Women must be really crazy about you."

I sat on the bed thinking, one foot toying with a kitten that had appeared from somewhere. Maybe I should accept her offer, spend a couple of months there and use the time to decide what to do next. The kitten became over-playful and sank its little teeth into my big toe.

"Scat! Bite my toe off, would you?" I shooed it away. "Where's your mother live?"

"About 200 kilometres from here. It's a nice place. You'd be by yourself there and nobody would bother you. Don't dither about it, let's just go. I don't know what trouble you're in here — I'm not nosy — but I know that if you've got to get away you couldn't find a better place."

Perhaps it really would suit me, but there was just one thing.

"Listen, I don't have any money at the moment. How could we travel?"

"I've got some, don't worry."

"All right. But I'm going to pay you back."

"We'll settle up in the end. You can earn your keep by doing a few jobs for my mother — chopping wood and maybe fix the roof. She's too old, now, but she used to do everything for herself."

I kissed her.

"So when should we go?"

"Right away, with the first train. Let's see — it's 4.30 now, and the first train goes at 6.05. We could be there in a couple of hours."

"Okay, where are my trousers?"

She leapt out of bed and went to the chest of drawers.

"While you were asleep yesterday, I bought you one or two things."

She opened the drawer and handed me a bulky package. I undid it. Inside were new trousers, a pullover, underwear and a pair of very heavy shoes.

188

"You got these for me?"

"Who else?"

"Listen, thanks." I looked at her, puzzled. "But why? You don't have the money for this."

"I've got money." She winked. "That big boss I was telling you about — you know, the father of my son — well, he pays me. Secretly, so his old goat doesn't find out. Just so..." she hesitated, "Just so he can come round once a month."

I felt a twinge in my chest. Perhaps I was jealous over her. I couldn't believe it. I wondered how many men she must have had.

"So I've got money, see. You don't need to worry about that," she urged me, unaware of the thoughts in my head.

"Thanks, I need the clothes. I'll give you the money back as soon as I can and I'll do whatever needs doing for your mother," I said drily.

I got dressed. The things she had bought were simple but new and of good quality. There was nothing else I needed. I looked at myself in the mirror over the chest of drawers and saw her behind me. What could I expect of her? She had already done so much for me.

"You can get dressed, I'll go out."

I went to the door. Suddenly she came up to me and burst into tears.

"What's the matter?"

"Nothing, it's just that you talk to me like a lady, and nobody's ever talked to me like that before."

"Come on, now, stop it. Get dressed."

I went into the kitchen. It was still dark. I stood in the darkness, smoking.

"Come in, dear. I'm ready now."

I went into the room. She was dressed in the same good grey costume I had first seen her in, but now I noticed that the skirt was quite fashionable, with buttons along the rear seam. She was also wearing black patent pumps and carried her grey beret in her hand.

"You dress well," I said, drawing her to me gently. "Who taught you?"

"Nobody. I picked it up myself. Would you like some coffee or tea? There's plenty of time."

"No thanks, I never eat as early as this. We'll get some breakfast on the train."

"Then I'll go down to the station and get the tickets so we don't have to queue. We don't want them seeing you." I realized I did not deserve this concern. "You come along five minutes before the train leaves. Be there on the platform at six. Just slam the door behind you." She made to leave but halted in the doorway. "Oh, I nearly forgot." She went to the wardrobe, took out a package and handed it to me.

I opened it: it was my journal.

"I was going to dry and iron your jacket yesterday, and it fell out. Now don't fret — I'm not a great one for reading and I've not looked at it."

"I wasn't fretting. Off you go. I'll see you at six." She came up to me and gave me a hug and a kiss.

"You're a real sweetie, darling."

"Get on with you." Gently I disengaged myself and nudged her towards the door.

She left. I went to the window. The night was waning, the sky lightening and a yellowy-whitish strip of dawn was growing in the East. Morning came pale, hesitant. I sat down at the table and opened my exercise book. I had forgotten all about it. I began to leaf through the pages of my sad nightmare. I thought how wonderful it would be to get right out of Moscow, out into the country, go hunting, tend the horses and the cows, settle down with her. I was sure she would give up the game.

I found a pen and wrote in the date. The book was slightly damp from the night I had spent out in the rain, and the pages were turned over at the corners, but the writing was clear and the ink had not even run. I looked at my watch — there was enough time. It was only a ten minutes walk to the station and I decided to jot down the events of the last two days.

I don't know what came over me, but I began to write very fast, as though the end of the world was nigh. I didn't want to put it off till later; I felt I had to do it now. My mind worked at a feverish rate and for half an hour I scribbled without a pause, but at ten to six I had to stop. It was the morning hour, that greenish pre-dawn gloom when not a sound can be heard but life is awakening. I had to leave.

EPILOGUE

He thrust the manuscript under his pullover and went
out. Outside it was quiet, windless and almost light,
although the sun was not yet up. A silvery mist drifted
from the ground and the roadway glistened from the
recent rain. He breathed in the clean air and thought
how good it was to be free, just to walk this street like this
to know you were not being hunted and that you could go
wherever you wished.

There was no need to hurry. Now he could see that
it was a narrow little lane, almost unsurfaced, with
ramshackle little houses and blind-looking windows —
a real slum. The night she had brought him here, sick
and exhausted, he had noticed nothing of this. On one
side he counted six tottery wooden houses and on the
other there was nothing — just a gigantic heap of bricks,
twisted iron and rotten planks.

The station was crowded. Everyone in different kinds of clothing — some in raincoats, some in suits and some women still sported fur coats. As he hurried towards the platform, he noticed that two men in civilian clothes who had been standing reading newspapers had detached themselves and were following him. Must be heading for the same train — he pushed aside the more ominous possibility.

He stepped out briskly, passing people with suitcases and bundles, past the newspaper kiosks, the porters with their carts, children and dogs. Looking back, he saw that the same two men were still behind him. On reaching the barrier he saw her. She was standing staring into the crowd, looking for him. He tried to slip past without her noticing him. First he had to check whether the two men were really after him. She must not get involved in this business.

Reaching the end of the platform, he jumped down onto the track and walked along it. Turning, he realized they were after him; it was obvious. What a stupid idea to go to a station when they knew all about him: the escape, the stolen car, killing the police dog. Of course they would have their people posted at all the stations; why hadn't he thought of that? They should have hitch-hiked into the country. Now he must get away from the men; shake them off. She would not leave without him, of course. Would she realize he had not deceived her. He could not go back and warn her, or they would pick her up too. Get away from them first, then get back to her. After that they would find a more sensible way than the train.

He walked quickly along the track and turned off to the left, where some spare coaches were parked. But then he saw three more men coming towards him. They were in police uniform. He stopped and turned. The other two were closer now. He looked ahead. One of the policemen cupped his hands and shouted:

"Parkin, give yourself up! We've got a car waiting for you at the main entrance".

He paid no attention but dashed to the left, towards the parked coaches. Behind them there must be a way into the town; if only he could get off the tracks, he could easily lose himself in the crowd. But yet two more men emerged from behind the coaches. He stood still; yes, they had thought of everything.

The same policeman again cupped his hands and yelled.

"Don't make trouble! Come to the car! You can't get away".

Well, it could not get worse, he thought.

"I'm not giving in. You'll have to take me", he yelled back.

The pair that had come from the direction of the coaches had moved. The two behind and the three policemen on the track stood and waited. The two ahead must be the team briefed to take him in. They were big, but he reckoned he could take them. They tried to jump him, and he hurled them aside. The other three policemen ran to their aid. Now five of them surrounded him, and one pounced on him. A fury seized him and he began to smash into them. He laid three of them out on the ground and the two others backed off, afraid.

Near by gangers must have been mending the track, for sections of rail and crowbars were scattered all round. One of the men grabbed a bar and swung it at him. He dodged, but the second one rushed in. He caught him and tossed him over his shoulder; the man landed heavily on his head, groaned and lay still. Now he only had to grab the bar from the remaining man and he could easily settle with him. He had forgotten the two who had stood a short distance away observing this whole scene. Other people were running now, jumping down from the platform.

He faced the man with the crowbar and watched him closely, his eyes never leaving the weapon. Then, from behind, a woman's cry. As he turned towards the voice, something crashed down onto his head. Falling, he saw her. She was running towards him, shouting: "My darling!"

Lord, I never even asked her her name, he thought as he drifted down into some dark abyss. Thought crowded on thought. Sasha with his violin, as he had appeared on the stage. Suddenly his blue fingers loosened and the violin fell to the floor. Boomm! echoed a call from somewhere. Then came his friends: Max and Rolf. Where are they? What happened to them? His last thought returned to her ramshackle house where she had sheltered, tended and warmed him, given him hope and a reason to go on living.

He lay face up between the tracks in the quiet of the grey, soft morning. The cheap exercise book lay open, its pages fluttering. At last he was now left alone, dead and gone in the midst of this hostile world of the lame and the blind. The sun rose, and its dead yellow-marble disk lit up Moscow's Five-Stations Square.

195